FOAL

LOVE, Penelope

JOANNE ROCKLIN

AMULET BOOKS
NEW YORK

LOVE, Penelope

JOANNE ROCKLIN

Cataloging-in-Publication Data has been applied for and may be obtained from the Library of Congress.

ISBN 978-1-4197-2861-7

Text copyright © 2018 Joanne Rocklin
Illustrations copyright © 2018 Lucy Knisley
Book design by Siobhán Gallagher

Printed and bound in U.S.A.
10 9 8 7 6 5 4 3 2 1

Amulet Books are available at special discounts when purchased in quantity for premiums and promotions as well as fundraising or educational use. Special editions can also be created to specification. For details, contact specialsales@abramsbooks.com or the address below.

ABRAMS The Art of Books
195 Broadway, New York, NY 10007
abramsbooks.com

In Memory of Zoe. Those who knew
and loved her understand.

Dear You,

Mama is going to have a baby. That baby will be you.
Right now you are just a tiny poppy seed inside of her.

You look like this:

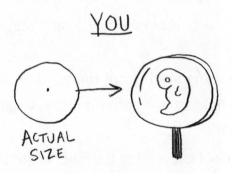

I have known about you for days. Mama and Sammy
had to tell me, because of all their happy hooting and
hollering.

Sammy said: "Don't tell anyone else about it yet." In
case you don't make it, You. But Mama says she doesn't
feel the same as those other times. She thinks you are
going to be fine.

But you are not an "it"!

You are a Somebody. You are a You.

Dear You.

You are a tiny speck inside Mama, but you are a speck of importance.

So hold on tight, You.

But here's the thing: When you are finally born, your age will be reset to zero! All that holding on and growing for nine months, as if it never happened.

Zero! Zilch! Nada!

You feel real to me right now. I can't stop thinking about you.

Mama saw me staring out the window. She said: "Your bran flakes have gotten mushy. What's going on with you?"

So I told her I had a lot of thoughts about the world and maybe I should write them down. I always feel better when I write things down.

And Mama went to her wobbly little kitchen desk and pulled out this fat notebook from the messy top drawer. As if she had been saving it just for me. It has a golden retriever on the cover, my favorite breed of dog, so cheerful and loving.

Mama said, "Here you go, Penny."

Mama understands how sometimes my thoughts sprout like little green shoots in my brain, squishing out words that could be used for normal conversation.

But Sammy knows a thing or two about me, too.

Sammy: "Whoa, maybe don't write about the whole WORLD, Penny. That's a lot. Don't overwhelm yourself."

I did feel a little whelmed when I saw the fat blank notebook. It is an awesome responsibility to introduce somebody to the world even though I didn't tell them I was writing to YOU, specifically.

Sammy continued: "Just get some words down, hon. Write about your own world, a little bit more each time. The things that are important to you and what's on your mind."

My OWN world. Phew! Because THEIR world is big and has wars and angry protests and elections and things like that in it.

OK, I think I can write some words to you about my own world.

I know reams about *you* already. That's because I am following your progress in Mama's book *What to Expect When You're Expecting*. There are lots of details in that book about all your growing activity, week by week and month by month. According to the book, at your age, less than a month old, you are now officially known as a BLASTOCYST. Blastocyst! What a fancy word for teeny-tiny you!!!

Words are so interesting to me. It is kind of wonderful that a bunch of alphabet letters arranged in different combinations can make you have different thoughts and feelings.

Words such as *rain*, R-A-I-N, make you feel good after a dry spell like we're having in California.

But not P-A-I-N, for example.

Also, when words are true, they are facts. When they are not true, they are lies. Or stories.

It's complicated.

And when words float along with musical notes, they are songs. We can harmonize, Mama, Sammy, and I. We do have room for a fourth singer.

You.

I just realized that W-O-R-L-D has the word *word* in it, when you cross out the *L*. That probably means something important, but I'm not going to try to figure it out at the moment.

I have to go to sleep now. Good night, Speck. Hold on tight. Remember, I am rooting for you.

Eight months until you are born, so eight months to write in this journal! Phew! But I vow to do it for you.

Love,

Penny

Dear You,

How great to be you! No worries. Nothing to do except grow inside Mama.

I have worries.

Sometimes they don't feel so little.

One worry is a heritage project I have to do for school, about where my family lived before they came to California.

I should be working on it right now. I am off from school for Thanksgiving and have some extra hours. We have a whole school year to do the project, which sounds like a lot of time, but we have to do something every month or so. Our teacher, Mr. Chen, is training us to do a big project in small bits, which is a very mature thing to learn how to do, now that we are in fifth grade.

But I will tell you that my project got off to a rocky start because there was a minor FABRICATION involving my teacher.

Well, my teacher didn't fabricate. I did.

A fabrication has nothing to do with fabric or clothes, You. It basically means that I lied about something.

Correction: My fabrication wasn't so minor.

Another worry involves the new girl, Hazel Pepper. She is an annoying BRAGGART. In other words, she brags.

My best friend, Gabby, doesn't agree that Hazel is an annoying braggart. This bothers me, because Gabby and I have agreed about every single thing for a long, long time, ever since Gabby's family moved to our street when we were both in first grade.

For example, Gabby and I agree that the Golden State Warriors is the greatest basketball team in the NBA. On the planet, probably! We call them the "Dubs," short for that *W* in *Warrior*. Golden State stands for the state of California, because we get a lot of golden sun.

Hazel is from Colorado, and she supports the Denver Nuggets.

By the way, I know you can't read this, little Speck. Except whenever I write the word *You*, it feels like you are listening. Right this minute.

Of course, you're not.

But it feels like it.

I don't have time to write more about my worries right now, because I have to start working on my school project.

Anyway, today is Thanksgiving Day, and I should be

writing about things I am thankful for, not things I am worried about.

We are having a fifteen-pound turkey with Sammy's cornbread stuffing and cranberry-orange relish. By the time you are born, you will probably weigh about half that, and that's pretty big for a former poppy seed. I am celebrating every one of your days on Earth today. Even if those days don't count officially.

Sammy is calling me for Thanksgiving dinner now. Oh, well. No time left to work on my project today.

Hold on, Speck.

Your sister,

Me, Penny

PS. I did tell Gabby my secret about you being in our lives.

(PS stands for POST (after) SCRIPT (my writing).)

LATER, SAME NIGHT

PPS. WOW! I just took a few minutes to figure out something amazing! You will be born this summer, soon after the Golden State Warriors win the National Basketball Association finals! The Warriors haven't won since 1975, when Gabby and I were MINUS twenty-nine years old!!!! (Hee-hee.) We will all be celebrating like crazy!

Many superstitious fans would never make a flat-out prediction about the Warriors' win, but Gabby and I are NOT superstitious.

So I think I will also use this journal to record the Dubs' march to victory. That way, you will be able to appreciate their victory when you are a Dubs fan, too, You.

> Warriors beat the Orlando Magic last night 111–96! And the night before, we beat the Miami Heat, because Steph Curry scored 40 POINTS!

FRIDAY, NOVEMBER 28, 2014

Dear You,

I know a lot about you from that book I told you about. But you don't know that much about me.

So.

I am Penelope Victoria Bach.

Nobody in our family is related to Johann

Sebastian Bach, a German composer from the eighteenth century. You will find out about him one day. His music is CLASSICAL. There are many different kinds of music, for example RAP, HIP-HOP, POLKA, and others that I don't have time to get into right now because of my heritage project.

Which I am about to work on.

Anyway, we're not related to that Bach. Sorry to digress. DIGRESS means to go off the subject.

In about half a year, I will be eleven years old. OK, I'm still ten. My birthday is coming up in May.

I've been told that I sometimes seem beyond my years because of my vocabulary and how I express myself. I hang around adults a lot. But I do not appear beyond my years physically. I actually appear below my years physically. The word for that is SHORT (compared to other fifth graders). I am hoping that will change in the near future, especially for basketball reasons. I'm a good dribbler, but not a good shooter, mostly because I am so short. Gabby and I are working on our shooting skills. We have a hoop in the driveway.

I will now attempt a drawing of myself, below. I am not that good an artist.

Anyway, here's me:

I actually don't understand why I'm not a better artist. I practice a lot. I have asked Mama and Sammy to buy me a set of colored pencils for Christmas. Professional quality.

The new girl, Hazel Pepper, can draw anything she wants without practicing at all. She says she feels incredibly blessed that she has that talent, because a picture can say a thousand words.

I don't know why she's worried about those thousand words. Hazel Pepper talks all the time.

Mama says everyone has her own gifts, and words can paint pictures just as well as colored pencils and markers and paint. The right words can have amazing power, Mama always says.

I guess I agree with her, because you can't really tell from the above drawing that I am not tall.

Or that I have a cowlick at the back of my head that sticks out like a chicken feather (unless I brush really hard).

Or that I like lots of people, except braggarts . . . not so much. Or that I like to read. And sing songs. Or that I play the ukulele in our school ukulele band. (Ukuleles are hard to draw.)

The only thing you can tell about me is that I'm a Golden State Warriors fan.

But everyone thinks Hazel Pepper's drawings are so awesome! I sound jealous. Really, I'm not.

Maybe a little bit.

As I said, Hazel Pepper is a Nuggets fan because she moved here from Colorado. I told her that Nuggets always makes me think of chicken nuggets (hee-hee).

I hate it when somebody doesn't laugh at a joke. Hazel Pepper didn't even crack a smile. She just replied that now that she lives in Oakland, she will work hard on changing her allegiance and learning about the Golden State Warriors. She said she has an excellent memory and it won't be hard.

Gabby said she would lend her a book about the Warriors and that her brother, Mike, has some extra posters of the players for Hazel Pepper's room. Hazel Pepper said she would also study about them online.

You can't just learn about the Dubs by reading! You have to have been watching them play for a lot of your life.

Forgot to work on my project again.

> Tonight, the Warriors beat the
> Charlotte Hornets, 106–101!!!
> Marreese Speights got hot with
> twenty-seven points!

Love,
Your sibling,
Penny

SAME DATE, EXTRA THOUGHTS BEFORE BED

Dear You,
PENNY is my NICKNAME, short for Penelope.

Nicknames are supposed to be "fun" names, but I like Penny for more than fun reasons.

It is a relief to be called Penny, because then I don't have to explain how my real name, PENELOPE, is spelled.

And I don't have to say, no, Penelope is not supposed to be pronounced like *cantaloupe*.

And I don't have to say that it is pronounced "PEN-EL-O-PEE." Sometimes, highly immature individuals make remarks (OK, laugh) about that last syllable. So that is another reason I like to be called Penny. When I, myself, was immature, a while ago, I used to punch people out for laughing at that last syllable.

Well, not that long ago and not that many people. Fourth grade and Kenny Walinhoff. And I only TRIED to punch him, because I missed.

When I told Mama and Sammy about that incident, they said Kenny was probably teasing me because he likes me. I don't mean to criticize our parents, You, but sometimes they think ILLOGICALLY.

That's it for now.

I have so much to talk to you about.

PS. I do have a secret impossible love. Maybe I will reveal it to you one day.

Dear You,

Mama's name is Becky, short for Rebecca.

Sammy's name is short for Samantha.

We have two mamas, You. And I love them both the same.

Sammy adopted me when I was a toddler. I started off calling her Sammy when I was little, and it stuck. If I called her Mama or even Mom, we would all get a little mixed up.

Did you know all this already? It feels like you did. But let me tell you more about our family anyway.

Mama and Sammy are called "domestic partners." They were once allowed to get married legally in California, but they didn't get around to it. And then the government said they were no longer allowed to, so they missed their chance. Then they were allowed to again. But, by that time, they'd decided that they were tired of listening to the government tell them what they were allowed to do.

Sometimes, I wish Mama and Sammy would get married. But they always say they have a "marriage of the heart," and that is just fine with them.

Mama is a college history professor. HISTORY

means the story of what happened. Sammy stays home and works on websites. I will explain what a WEBSITE is one day. It's complicated, Speck.

Mama was an orphan who was raised by several foster families in the little town of Junoville, Wyoming. Mama married another orphan, my daddy, William Wolney.

It's kind of romantic that two orphans fell in love.

Mama says my dad was a friendly guy with a big smile and a gap between his two front teeth. I have a photo of him and Mama on the motorcycle they rode on, all the way to Oakland from Wyoming, for Mama's job.

Then they had me. Then my dad crashed that motorcycle on Highway 24.

And, sadly, he died.

I don't remember my dad at all. Mama doesn't like to talk about their lives in Junoville. I guess it's pretty sad to think about one's orphaned fate. My own memories are all of Mama and Sammy Bach.

Here is a drawing of Mama and Sammy:

They look much, much better in real life, which you will see for yourself eventually.

Love,

Me, Penny

PS. Sammy has lots of relatives here in Oakland. Many of Sammy's relatives have been here forever. Ohlone forever. OH-LO-NEE. As in native Californian. Sammy is 50 percent Ohlone.

When I was in third grade, we first learned about the Ohlone, who have lived in this area for thousands of years. They are real Californians—more than anybody else who came later. I hadn't realized how cool it was, having an Ohlone family member. Now I do.

Dear You,

Oakland is my city, and yours, too, in an inside-somebody-else kind of way. Gabby and I think the Golden State Warriors should be called the Oakland Warriors because they play right here in Oracle Arena. Except we call it "ROARACLE Arena." Oakland fans really ROAR! We are the best fans in the world.

Mama and Sammy are not basketball fans. That's their biggest flaw, IMHO (In My Humble Opinion). Other than that, they're pretty cool. They are fans of other things, such as blues music and golf and *Antiques Roadshow* on PBS.

I am hoping you will be a basketball fan, You. Actually, I just know you will. I will inspire you. It's lonely being the only fan in this house. Gabby and her older brother, Mike, watch games together all the time. She got her basketball enthusiasm from Mike and passed it on to me.

Mama and Sammy say I shouldn't care so much about winning. Admission: I hate to say this about our own parents, You, but that is HYPOCRITICAL of them. Hypocritical is when you say you believe something but you act like you don't.

For example, when there's an exciting Dubs game on (like tonight when we beat the Detroit Pistons 104–93), and there's a lot of hooting and hollering from yours truly, Mama and Sammy will slide into the room at the very end, just to see who wins, because that's all they care about. They skip all the other good stuff leading up to the end. How weird is that? But true fans, such as me and Gabby, and her brother, Mike, root for our team from beginning to end, through up and down, thick or thin, and everywhere in between.

Go Dubs!

Your sib,

Penny

MONDAY, DECEMBER 1, 2014

Dear You,

As I said, our family lives in OAKLAND, a city in California.

The following information is important, You.

Do NOT get fooled when you hear someone talk about the City when they are really talking about SAN FRANCISCO, which is across the Bay. I don't get fooled. I just get angry.

Here are those cities on a little map of California:

See? Two stars on a map. Two different cities. There should be no "the" in their descriptions at all. I ABHOR that! Oakland's a fine city. It is not a watered-down San Francisco! But, sometimes, even Oaklanders call San Francisco "the City"!

SIX GREAT THINGS ABOUT OAKLAND, CALIFORNIA:

1. It has its very own lake. Not every city does.
2. It has Jack London Square, where Gabby and I pretend we own the fancy yachts docked there. One for each of us.
3. It has cool hipsters who wear whatever they want, spiky blue or green or any color hair and tall furry boots and dark-tinted sunglasses. And tattoos. Gabby and I plan on getting tattoos as soon as we're allowed. Probably not in the near future.

4. Food!!!!!!! Tall, tall ice cream sundaes at Fentons, and markets with lots of free samples where you can buy food from all around the world: Hup Seng cream crackers and tostados and samosas and sushi—you name it!
5. Even our graffiti is spectacular—striped like candy and glittery like fireworks.
6. And the Oakland A's and the Oakland Raiders AND the Golden State Warriors. How cool is all that?

CORRECTION: That's eight great things about Oakland, if you were counting.

Oakland used to have many more oak trees than it has now. That's where it gets its name. The Ohlone used to make meals from the acorns of the oak trees.

Anyway, I am digressing.

OK, I'm not really digressing. Acorns and the Ohlone have something to do with my terrible FABRICATION. I guess it is time to tell you about it.

Tomorrow.

Love,

Penny

PS. You have a new name! You are now at 4 weeks and are called an EMBRYO.

Dear You,

Here it is, THE STORY ABOUT MY TERRIBLE FABRICATION.

First of all, I have to tell you that Mr. Chen is my favorite of all the teachers I've ever had in my life. I like him because he wears a different tie almost every day.

I know that good taste in ties is a minor reason to like your teacher, but I am positive he chooses his ties carefully, with his students in mind. Teachers aren't even required to wear ties. Mr. Chen's ties give us something interesting to look at when our minds wander or just because.

I truly believe that says a whole lot about a teacher.

Here are just a few of the ties he has worn so far:

His Müller-Lyer Optical Illusion Tie

Surprise! If you measure those two lines they are the same exact size! Really!

Here are a few more:

And also, Mr. Chen's eyes look at everyone in a kind way.

I really, really want Mr. Chen to like me. He seems to like me, but if he ever finds out that I'm a fabricator, I don't think he will.

Anyway, here's the story.

Mr. Chen told us about the heritage project a month before I began this journal.

Kids who live in Oakland, in all of California, actually, often have interesting heritages. Many people from around the world have come to live in our state because of our freedoms.

And, of course, the nice weather.

Mr. Chen reminded us that most American families came from somewhere else. The United States has always been a nation of immigrants. Mr. Chen feels that remembering this fact is extremely important. All of my teachers have thought it was important. So I have had to draw many family trees over the years, although my trees are always kind of bare.

The first part of Mr. Chen's project is to write a simple three-to-four-sentence paragraph about our families' origins. But there will be other parts, he said. He gave us a project sheet to share with our parents. We should try to hand in something every month.

The project will CULMINATE with an oral presentation, and that's when all the project parts come together. I'm not thrilled about that oral presentation, even though mine would be short and easy. But boring.

Mr. Chen told us that his own ancestors came to California from China to help build the Central Pacific Railroad.

Amir told the class that his grandfather came from Calcutta in India.

Sophia's parents came separately from Turkey and fell in love right here in Oakland.

Gabby's parents came from Jamaica with her brother, Mike, before Gabby was born.

Antonio's parents came from Arizona and Mexico.

Issa's parents came from Texas and Kenya.

Hazel Pepper's mother came from Russia and her father came from England.

And, of course, she went on and on for a thousand words or so until Mr. Chen kindly interrupted her "to let someone else speak."

I thought everyone's stories were so wonderful!

Before I knew it, my brain began imagining an "impress Mr. Chen story" about my own heritage, except it was someone else's heritage. And I hadn't planned to share it out loud.

Until I raised my hand.

Me: "My ancestors were always, always here. They didn't ARRIVE from anywhere. They were already here!"

"With the dinosaurs?" Kenny Walinhoff called out. Ha ha. Several kids laughed as if that was the funniest joke they'd ever heard.

Mr. Chen frowned at them. Then he gave me his "I'm SO VERY interested" look. (His forehead goes up and his eyes kind of beam sparkles at you.)

"Tell us more, Penelope," he said. Even the little dancing snowmen on the tie he was wearing that day seemed interested.

Here comes the fabrication.

Me: "I am descended from a native Californian tribe. The Ohlone, to be specific."

There. I'd said it. The story had traveled from my brain, down to my tongue, and out of my mouth, and when it hit air, it became a fabrication. Another word for that is LIE.

Me: "And princesses."

Of course there had to be princesses.

Not the timid kind with gold crowns and purple-pink gowns and uncomfortable pointy slippers.

No. The brave kind with clothes made of animal skins. There were probably bare feet involved, too, swift and speedy feet that never left a mark as they pad-padded among the oak trees. I was looking down at my sneakers. I was imagining muddy toes.

"Penny?"

I looked up. I wasn't sure how long I had been pad-padding among the oak trees.

Mr. Chen: "I'm wondering whose side of the family."

"My mother's side," I said.

And now you know, You. I do feel bad about the borrowed heritage, but it is too late to turn back.

Is it really too late to turn back? I mean, is it too late to tell Mr. Chen the truth?

Gabby knows I told a lie. She knows that Sammy is not my biological mother and that I borrowed her heritage. Gabby said she understands why I did it, on account of my usually bare and boring family trees.

She promised to keep my fabrication a secret, because that's what friends are for.

I told her it did feel pretty good to borrow Sammy's heritage for a few minutes.

Anyway, that's the fabrication.

I am happy to be able to write about all this to you, even though I don't feel happy about borrowing Sammy's heritage anymore.

Your sibling,

Penny

PS. I do not plan to share the project sheet with Mama and Sammy. I will paste it in here for ready reference. Mama and Sammy believe in privacy and told me they would never peek in this private journal. Mama and Sammy always tell the truth.

We beat the Magic again!
Whew! Close. 98–97.

PROJECT SHEET

In just a few sentences, tell us where members of your family lived before they came to California. Perhaps you weren't even born yet! You can describe one or both sides of your family—it is your choice.

- Does your family have any artifacts or dress items that relate to your heritage?

- Are there ceremonies, customs, or rituals associated with your heritage?

- What was the language of your family's place of origin? Do you know some words in that language?

- Are there specific foods associated with your family's heritage? Share a recipe if you can.

- Interview a family member about what your heritage means to him or her.

- Tell us something about the history of the country or state you came from.

CULMINATION: Plan an oral presentation combining the information you gathered about your heritage. You can bring any visual aids you'd like.

Dear You,

RELATIVE is another excellent word to know. It refers to people who are in your family.

But it can also mean one thing compared to another thing.

For example, I am old, relative to you.

The Earth is big, relative to a raindrop.

The Earth is small, relative to the whole starry universe.

I like to remember that word RELATIVE when I shoot baskets.

Let me explain what I mean:

Today after school, Gabby and I were watching a bunch of kids play HORSE. Kids at our school love that game and play it rain or shine. As a matter of fact, it was raining today, and they were still playing it!

It's an easy enough basketball game, You.

Everyone stands in a line. The first player gets to do any crazy thing they want before they shoot. Hop up and down. Whistle. Turn around three times. If they make their shot, the others have to do the exact same thing. If the first person misses that shot, the next person gets to make up a crazy shot for the others to copy. Anyone who misses a person's crazy shot, gets the letter *H*. You just keep playing like this and when you get enough misses to spell HORSE you are O-U-T. The last one left who did not yet spell HORSE is the winner.

I don't know what it's like at other schools, but at Pacific Beach Elementary School, you will notice something peculiar.

Me: "Did you ever notice that only the boys are playing HORSE? That's SEXISM."

Gabby: "No. It's not sexism if the girls don't join in!"

Hmmm, I thought. *She's so right*. So, today, we did.

At first, the boys looked surprised when we stood in line to play.

Kenny Walinhoff to me: "You're too short for basketball."

Gabby: "She is a bit short, but not TOO short. Steph Curry is short, too, and look at him!"

Kenny: "Steph Curry is NOT short! He's six foot three. You call that short?"

Me: "Yes. Because it's all RELATIVE, like Aunty Lue in her yellow convertible."

Kenny: "Huh?"

But Gabby knew just what I meant. Sometimes, Gabby and I can read each other's minds. High fives!

So Gabby told Kenny about her aunty Lue, formerly from Chicago, who always drives her car with the top rolled down, almost all the time. Her aunty Lue says the weather is warm here, compared to Chicago.

Gabby: "See? It's all relative."

Me: "And Steph Curry is short if you compare him to Draymond Green, who is six foot seven. And how about Andrew Bogut, who is seven feet? So Curry tries harder and constantly practices his three-pointers."

Everybody in back of us in line was getting impatient. "Come on, come on, start the game!" one boy yelled.

Kenny wriggled his nose three times, then made the shot.

I was next. I was going to give it my all. It's all relative, relative, relative, I thought.

I wriggled my nose three times.

Just then, Kenny Walinhoff asked me if I was ever going to tell Mr. Chen my "real" name. Pen-el-o-pee-pee.

And I missed my shot for an *H*.

It would have been really easy to punch Kenny, but I decided to be the mature one in the situation. Except that I didn't feel like playing HORSE anymore, which really wasn't very mature at all.

On the way home, Gabby said kindly, "I like your

name, Penelope. It sounds like a name from the British TV show *Downton Abbey.*"

Can you see why she is my best friend, You? My name sounded pretty when she said it.

But there was Hazel, walking home with us. She's been doing that lately. Her street is around the corner from ours.

Hazel: "I like your name, too, Penelope. It sounds like a little drum roll. Rah-TAT-a-tat! Pen-EL-o-pe!"

Gabby and Hazel both started singing: "Rah-TAT-a-tat! Pen-EL-o-pe! Rah-TAT-a-tat! Pen-EL-o-pe!" dancing to that rhythm all the way down the block. They didn't even notice I wasn't joining in.

Nobody will make fun of YOUR name, You. I solemnly promise. As soon as I find out what your name will be, before it is announced to the world and too late to change, I will check it upside down and inside out. Just to make sure.

Your sibling,

Pen

FRIDAY, DECEMBER 5, 2014

Dear You,

We are so glad for the rain this week because

California is experiencing a terrible drought. There hasn't been enough winter rain to water the farmers' crops. I worry about our drought.

You yourself are a water baby! I read that you are surrounded and cushioned by fluid inside Mama's uterus. That is wondrous to me. *What to Expect* says you even look like a little tadpole. And you have a tiny tail!

Everything about you is wondrous to me.

Love,

Penny

Last night we beat the New Orleans Pelicans 112–85. Yes!

SATURDAY, DECEMBER 6, 2014

Dear You,

Uncle Ziggy came by tonight.

Uncle Ziggy is Sammy's younger brother. Ziggy is a nickname, short for Zachariah.

You will notice that Uncle Ziggy is over here a lot.

I have a feeling that Mama and Sammy have him over to make sure I have an important male figure in my life because I have two moms. I don't even think about that, even though he IS important to me. I just love Uncle Ziggy. He is funny and kind.

He always brings his ukulele for after-dinner sing-alongs. He is a troubadour, he says, which is a singing poet, although he's had a lot of other jobs. Uncle Ziggy has a beautiful, trembly voice, halfway between a country singer and a rock star. I play my ukulele with him even though I only know a few chords. But we all sing loudly, and it covers up my bloopers.

Uncle Ziggy is hard at work looking for a high-paying job that will still give him time for troubadouring. But when he is not looking for a high-paying job, he is mapping out secret stairways. Uncle Ziggy belongs to the Oakland Secret Stairway Society (OSSS). That's another great thing about Oakland. There are many secret stairways because the city is so hilly. The stairways hide behind alleys or pop up at the end of paths. Some lead to gardens. Some lead to other stairways. The mysterious ones just stop and lead nowhere.

Mama and Sammy think his job search is leading nowhere, so we are helping him spruce up his RESUME (rez-oo-MAY). Resume is another word for "list of jobs you have had in your life." In Uncle Ziggy's case, it's not that many high-paying ones.

Uncle Ziggy: "This is my resume." He picked up his uke, and I plunked along with him on mine.

(To the tune of "I've Been Working on the Railroad.")
I've been working as a supermarket checker,
A painter and a whaddya-call-it,
A clown and a sailor and an auto wrecker,
Just to get some dollars in my wallet.

You will love Uncle Ziggy, too.

Uncle Ziggy is a devoted Warriors fan, like I am. He knows a lot about basketball. But he is one of those Extremely Superstitious Fans. He always wears a Warriors shirt when he watches a game, even when he's alone in his apartment, he says. And the same pair of blue socks, even if he's worn them for other games without washing them first. Possibly the same underwear, too.

> Tonight, we beat the Chicago Bulls, 112–102! Our twelfth straight victory, and we weren't even playing at home!

Your sib,
Penny

SUNDAY, DECEMBER 7, 2014

Dear You,

Am I becoming superstitious like Uncle Ziggy? I woke up this morning feeling like all the colors of the rainbow at once because of our basketball wins. I was positive something nice was going to happen today. And something did!

Gabby and I were in Gabby's driveway, practicing our shots. Mike came out of the house, and Gabby asked him to give us some tips. He agreed right away. The tips were awesome.

He told us to keep our eyes up whenever we dribbled. He also had us do a shooting drill to help get the same backspin on the ball as Curry does.

Mike: "Imagine a cookie jar filled with your favorite cookies. It's sitting on a very high shelf. Now reach your arm up, up, up, as high as you can to reach the jar, and then bend your hand to grab a cookie inside. Now, try the same motion except, this time, with a ball in your hand."

I imagined Mama's chocolate chip cookies with hazelnuts. Mike's tip really works! With the ball in your hand, when you reach into the imaginary cookie jar, the ball spins perfectly off your fingertips!

Then Mike called us the Splash Sisters. That's what everyone calls the Dubs' Steph Curry and Klay Thompson—but, of course, they call them the Splash Brothers. We laughed, but it did feel good when he called us that.

By the way, Mike's voice sounds like he's about to burst into song. Also, Mike has Quiet Confidence and doesn't brag.

Love,

Penny

SUNDAY, DECEMBER 14, 2014

Dear You,

Lots of rain this week. We hope we get much more.

I haven't written in a while because I lost this journal when I accidentally dropped it into the laundry basket. But I was happy to find You again, Speck, especially right before Blue Monday.

Sometimes our family gets the blues on Monday morning, having to start the week all over again. Especially if the weekend was fun. In our home, we believe in fighting the Monday blues.

THREE WAYS TO FIGHT THE MONDAY BLUES

1. Wear something in the blue category. Royal blue, turquoise, navy blue, baby blue—it doesn't matter. Seriously, this helps cheer you up when you are feeling "blue." It does for our family, anyway.

2. Do the laundry Sunday night. (That's how I found this journal again.) Mama does the whites, I do the colors, and Sammy folds. We'll have to find a job for you, You. That way everyone has nice fresh clothes Monday morning to start off the week.

3. Have Sundae Mondays to look forward to after Monday dinner. Mama and Sammy and I are crazy for ice cream.

There is always a flavor of the month. This month's is Rum Raisin, even though I have a feeling real rum isn't involved. Then we pile on fixings, which are set out on the table: gummy bears, sprinkles, crumbled Oreo cookies, the usual stuff.

I can't wait to introduce you to Sundae Mondays! You will be crazy for them. But I guess you will first have to go through the warm-milk and mixed-vegetable baby food stages. Ugh. (Sorry.)

Anyway, there are a few things I'm a teeny bit blue about, and it's not even Monday yet.

Hazel Pepper walked over after school on Friday. Gabby and I were shooting baskets in the driveway.

Hazel Pepper: "Happy Andrew Bogut Day!"

Gabby: "Thanks!"

Friday was December 12, and twelve is Andrew Bogut's number on his team jersey. When we remember to do it, Gabby and I celebrate some of our favorite Dubs on the days of the month that are the same number as their jersey numbers. It's a private thing.

But not private anymore, I guess.

Gabby looked at me SHEEPISHLY. Sheepishly has nothing to do with sheep, You. It just means you are a bit embarrassed, for example, when you blab about something you and your best friend made up for fun.

I don't know if sheep get especially embarrassed, but there you go.

So here is something to be cheerful about: The Warriors have had a sixteen-game winning streak! How long can a winning streak last?

> 12/8/14 v Minnesota
> Timberwolves 102–86; 12/10/14
> v Houston Rockets 105–93;
> 12/13/14 v Dallas Mavericks,
> 105–98; 12/14/14 v New Orleans
> Pelicans 128–122.

Gabby said Mike said we have a long way to go to beat the NBA record of thirty-three, set by the 1971–72 Los Angeles Lakers. It is time to break that record!

Mike knows so much.

Love, me,

Penny

MONDAY, DECEMBER 15, 2014

Dear You,

This afternoon, I practiced my jumping. I stand next to the wall near our garage with some chalk. I hold the chalk high and jump hard. I pretend my legs are coiled-up springs. *Sprong!* Then I make a chalk mark as high as I can. Know what? I'm getting better all the time, because the chalk marks end up higher and higher.

Later, Gabby and I were in my driveway, and wouldn't you know it, there was Kenny Walinhoff, walking down the block across the street.

Sprong! I jumped, and the ball went into the cookie jar! Usually, Gabby and I disdainfully ignore Kenny, but this time we didn't.

"It's all relative!" we shouted.

Kenny crossed the street. "You're right," he said.

Gabby: "Of course we're right."

Kenny: "Do you know about Muggsy Bogues? And also Spud Webb? They are retired players. They were great even though they were short. You should know about them."

Me, disdainfully: "Who says I don't know about them?"

Actually, I didn't know about Spud Webb. But still.

Me, after Kenny left: "Kenny thinks he knows everything about basketball!"

Gabby: "I think he likes you. I always see him looking at you. Do you like him back?"

Me: "Don't be silly. He infuriates and humiliates me. He is so immature."

Gabby: "But I see you looking at him, too."

Me: "Disdainfully. Anyway, I DO like someone, but it's not Kenny."

Those words had been just a secret impossible feeling inside my heart, and in my journal to you, until I said them out loud.

Of course Gabby wanted to know who that secret someone was. We have always told each other everything. I said I couldn't tell her at the moment. She said she would respect my privacy.

I don't want to tell anyone. Not even you, You. Yet.

Love,

Penny

WEDNESDAY, DECEMBER 17, 2014

Dear You,

I am flabbergasted.

FLABBER-GASTED.

I love that word. It sounds just like I feel. I don't like the way I feel, though.

And why am I flabbergasted?

Because the Warriors LOST to the Memphis Grizzlies last night, that's why!!! Score: 98–105.

I had an argument with Mama and Sammy tonight when I told them why I was flabbergasted and that our winning streak was over.

Mama, in a crabby voice: "That's the way the ball bounces, hon."

Me, also crabby: "That is NOT the way the ball bounces. Usually, the ball bounces to Steph Curry, and he makes all his threes. He lost two three-pointers back-to-back in the game's final ten seconds!"

At least she didn't ask who Steph Curry is like she always does, so I didn't have to explain, once again, for the zillionth time, that he's the Dubs' wonderful, stupendous point guard.

Mama was munching a Fig Newton. She eats them when she is nauseated. "That's the way the cookie crumbles, then. A loss had to happen sooner or later."

"Cookies crumbling! Balls bouncing! Ha ha!" I said. "Your metaphors need improving!"

"Cool it, Pen," said Sammy in a soft voice.

Mama: "It's just a game, Penny."

My lip was trembling. I almost began crying like a baby. Like you will be crying soon, Speck, except you'll be crying for food, or a dry diaper, or for no reason at all, I guess.

But I had a reason, except it was so hard to explain with words, even though I tried.

Me: "It is NOT just a game. It's the Dubs! It's Oakland's team!"

And then something happened that you will find amazing, sib. I find it amazing, every time.

Mama looked at Sammy. Sammy looked at Mama. THEN THEY READ EACH OTHER'S MIND. Gabby says her parents can do that, too.

Sammy: "The Dubs are important to you. We should respect that."

Mama: "Yes, we should. I apologize, kiddo. You love your city, and you love your Dubs."

Mama and Sammy hugged me, and we all sat on the couch together, munching on Fig Newtons. They were trying so hard to be understanding. That was very kind of them. I don't think they really understand, though.

But I felt better when we started planning our big family Christmas dinner. And peace on earth, goodwill toward men and women, stuff like that.

And we talked about you.

I have no hard feelings that you have made Mama feel nauseated and throw up every now and then. And maybe a little bit crabby. That's the way the cookie crumbles when a mama is pregnant (hee-hee).

You are 10,000 times bigger than you were when you were just a speck! According to *What to Expect*, you are now the size of a blueberry.

By the way, this is what you look like around now, below.

I copied it out of *What to Expect*. You are not a pretty sight, with that big, weird head. Good job making sure your brain develops right away, though. And I know you'll be just as cute as can be by the time you arrive.

But you are beginning to grow tiny arms and legs, ears, a mouth, and intestines. You have a beating heart. It's miraculous.

Love,

Penny

12/18/14: We beat the Oklahoma City Thunder 114–109.

Dear You,

We have begun winter break.

Yay! Drizzles of rain! We need the rain.

And another win for the Dubs!

Tonight, 128–108 v the Sacramento Kings.

Hazel came over. She brought homemade bookmarks with portraits of her favorite Dubs as Christmas gifts for me and Gabby.

I think Steph Curry has flatter ears than she drew for him, and Klay Thompson's beard should have gone all the way around his mouth and chin. But, OK, her gift was thoughtful.

Love,

Pen

THURSDAY, DECEMBER 25, 2014

Dear You,

Happy Christmas! Your first one on earth!

For Christmas dinner, we squished eleven people around our table—and one dog under it—me, Mama, Sammy, Uncle Ziggy, Grandma Lorraine, Great-Grandma Grace; cousins Martha and Tony and Nelson; and Uncle Raymond and Aunt Faith. These are all relatives from Sammy's side of the family because my orphaned mother and deceased orphaned father never knew their relatives.

The dog was a white shih tzu named Frances who belongs to cousin Martha.

It was a happy and merry day and evening except for the fact that Uncle Ziggy dropped our dinner.

He was wearing bright-red-and-green shorts. And bright-red socks with green tassels on the cuffs, which may have been the problem. He was carrying the ham on a platter from the kitchen when, suddenly, Frances leaped out from under the table, snarling and yapping, and attacked Uncle Ziggy's ankles. He dropped the platter and . . . sprong, sprong, dribble! That ham bounced across the room, just like a basketball.

You could tell Uncle Ziggy felt awful. His face was almost as red as his socks. So people tried to make him feel better with jokes, and Uncle Ziggy joked, too, of course.

Uncle Ziggy: "Out of bounds!"

Sammy: "Luckily, our floors are so clean you can eat off of them!"

Mama quickly scooped the ham back onto the platter. She said: "Don't worry! We have another ham exactly like it in the kitchen. I'll be right back."

Dinner was yummy, especially the "new" ham (hee-hee).

I got several nice presents. My favorite is from Mama and Sammy—that big set of beautiful colored pencils, expensive professional quality. Just what

I asked for. I am sure they will vastly improve my drawing. I also got some very nice golden retriever stationery from Uncle Ziggy.

Confession: I was hoping with all my might that the Warriors would beat the Los Angeles Clippers. That would have been a great Christmas gift. They have lost three out of the last five games!

Steph Curry on TV: "We are NOT invincible."

He is so humble, a nice way to be. Especially on Christmas Day.

I should be feeling a lot of peace and goodwill and humbleness toward all people on Earth, including Clipper fans. The Clipper fans in Los Angeles deserved a win on Christmas, too.

Still.

Love,

Penny

Warriors lost to the Los Angeles Clippers 12/25/14, 86–100.

A win v the Minnesota Timberwolves 12/27/14, 110–97.

SUNDAY, DECEMBER 28, 2014

Dear You,

It is now a long, lazy afternoon. Mama is sleeping and Sammy is cooking chili. A good day to write to you, You.

Yesterday afternoon I asked Sammy to drop me off at Grandma Lorraine and Great-Grandma Grace's house while she and Mama went to the movies. They are Sammy's mom and grandmother, RESPECTIVELY. That word means "in the same order." It doesn't mean "respect," even though I do respect them.

Sammy knows that I love just hanging out with Grandma Lorraine and Great-Grandma Grace. But I also planned to get some information about Ohlone artifacts and rituals and ceremonies so that I could continue with my fabrication. Of course I wasn't going to tell them why I was so interested in all that, in case they told Mama and Sammy.

I learned much more than I thought I would. Much more. And I can't stop thinking about it.

You will like them both a lot. Grandma Lorraine Bach is skinny but strong and she runs the three miles around Lake Merritt every day. She often wears a T-shirt that says RUNNING IS MY HIGH.

Great-Grandma Grace is elderly, probably way over eighty, and proud of her age. She has wrinkles all over her face and arms, like spiderwebs, but her skin is velvet soft. She has long black hair, as black as a raven, as black as coal, as black as the deep, dark night. I can tell that she has never dyed her hair, because there are strands like silver threads running through it. (We are reviewing similes in class.)

Great-Grandma Grace has pretty designs of dots and lines on her chin in the traditional Ohlone way.

Both of them are 100 percent Ohlone. Sammy is only 50 percent because Grandma Lorraine married the late Mr. Henry Bach, who was German.

I decided to begin by asking about Ohlone ceremonies. I know that Grandma Lorraine likes to talk about her deceased husband, Mr. Bach. They were madly in love.

Me, casually: "When you got married to Henry Bach, what was your wedding ceremony like?"

Grandma Lorraine: "Um . . ."

Great-Grandma Grace: "Go on, tell her!"

Grandma Lorraine looked at me, well, sheepishly. "Henry and I ran off to Vegas. Elvis married us."

Me: "Elvis!"

Grandma Lorraine: "Or someone who sure looked

like him. He had big muttonchops and a white pant-suit with spangles and a red sparkly belt. The whole thing took about five minutes, and the Elvis guy played a guitar as we walked down the aisle. We were young and in a hurry, what can I say?"

So I decided to move on to precious artifacts of their Ohlone heritage. I knew for sure that Grandma Lorraine had a beautiful necklace made of shimmery abalone shells. She wears it when she gets dressed up. I asked her to show it to me because I love it so much, which is true. I even asked her to take a photo of it with her iPhone and print the photo for me, so I could show my best friend, Gabby.

Then I asked Great-Grandma Grace if she has an Ohlone artifact that is precious to her.

Great-Grandma Grace: "Well, MY precious artifact is a beautiful round red-and-white basket with green and red feathers and shiny abalone beads. Woven willow shoots and sedge roots and black triangles of fern roots make a pattern all around. The Ohlone had many uses for baskets, but their baskets were also works of art, made of of bits of the earth and the sea and the sky!" she said. "The most beautiful basket in the world."

Wowee. I couldn't wait to take a photo of the most

beautiful basket in the world, made of bits of the earth and the sea and the sky! But when I asked to see it, Great-Grandma Grace tapped the side of her head.

"My basket is a memory," she said. "A memory of a memory of a story about the basket. Memories and stories are just about the most precious things the Ohlone have left. We've lost a lot, Penny."

Grandma Lorraine: "Every year, the day after Thanksgiving, Mom and I go to the little memorial park at the corner of Ohlone Way and Shellmound Street in Emeryville. Do you know why we go there, Penny?"

I told her that once, when I was younger, I went to that park with Mama and Sammy. I remember the chanting and the drumming. I thought it was a celebration.

Grandma Lorraine: "Yes, that day is a celebration of our culture, but it is also a protest. That day you were standing on an ancient sacred site."

Then Grandma Lorraine told me something I can't stop thinking about. She said that there used to be a huge shell mound in that spot, a big tall mountain of shells from the shellfish the Ohlone ate. The shell mound was older than the pyramids of Egypt. It was a community ceremonial and trading spot and an area where the Ohlone buried their dead. Over the years, Americans destroyed that shell mound. They built one thing after another on top of it—an amusement park and a dance pavilion and railroad tracks and a paint factory. Today, streets and sidewalks and the gigantic Bay Street mall are on that sacred spot.

But here is the worst part:

Hundreds of bodies were dug up from their graves when construction workers were building the mall! Ancestors of the Ohlone who had been buried there for many, many years. Some of the skeletons are now in a museum. Others were left buried under the mall. And others were just thrown away!

Grandma Lorraine: "We begged the developers to leave it as a big, open space to honor our heritage, but nobody listened to us. It was a desecration."

A DESECRATION! When the early Ohlone buried their loved ones, they thought they would lie in that sacred spot for eternity!

Great-Grandma Grace: "So on the day after every Thanksgiving, as shoppers stroll by, we educate them about the history of that spot. Maybe we can prevent that desecration from happening again. From happening to anyone's heritage!"

Now I understand why Grandma Lorraine and Great-Grandma Grace never ever shop at that mall.

Love,

Penny

PS. I am wondering if it is too late to tell Mr. Chen the truth about a heritage that isn't mine at all.

THURSDAY, JANUARY 1, 2015

Dear You,

2015. Two thousand and fifteen.

Mama: "It has a turning-point sound."

She says that every year. Every New Year's date has a turning-point sound, because we're not used to saying it. So it sounds important.

But, of course, you are arriving this year, and that is a huge turning point for our family.

Love,

Pen

LATER, SAME NIGHT

PS. I made a solemn New Year's resolution for 2015: Always, always, always tell the truth.

Especially to you. That is my awesome responsibility. Why keep a journal if you aren't going to be completely honest and reveal all?

I keep thinking about the bodies buried under the Bay Street mall.

I plan to tell Mr. Chen the truth pretty soon. Borrowing (stealing!) a heritage that isn't mine is weighing heavily on my conscience.

Love,

Penelope

MONDAY, JANUARY 5, 2015

Dear You,

Back at school. Mr. Chen said that only one person hadn't turned anything in yet for our project, and that person knows who that person is.

Anyway, happy Sundae Monday. Caramel Cream Custard. Too sweet.

OK, I hereby vow in writing: IF THE WARRIORS WIN THREE MORE TIMES, I WILL TELL MR. CHEN THE ABSOLUTE TRUTH.

Love,

Me

SATURDAY, JANUARY 10, 2015

Dear You,

According to *What to Expect*, you have already graduated from being an embryo to being a FETUS. Congratulations! Your legs are developing bones and little dents for knees and ankles. It is time to call you Feet instead of Speck. Get ready for jumping, Feet!

Also, *What to Expect* points out that you have increased your size 300 percent, from one half inch at eight weeks to one and a half inches at ten weeks. In just two weeks! If that happened to me, I would be almost thirteen feet tall! I would be taller than the tallest Warrior!

Again, it's all relative.

You are working so, so hard to grow.

By the way, I'm not THAT superstitious, but there have been signs that it is time to tell Mr. Chen the truth.

SIGN #1: I have been searching high and low for my lucky plastic four-leaf clover for weeks and weeks. The other day, I found it stuck in a dust ball under my bed.

SIGN #2: Today, Mama said she could eat egg salad for the first time in weeks without feeling nauseated. Also, her heartburn is easing up.

SIGN #3: I saw two yellow banana slugs in the yard early this morning, side by side. It seems to me that banana slugs are solitary creatures and don't usually hang out in pairs. By the way, banana slugs are not easy to love, but they are easy to draw, even for me, and especially with my professional-quality pencils:

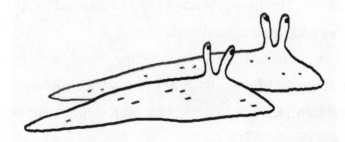

SIGN #4: Well, actually signs 4, 5, and 6. Three more Warriors wins! Of course I am happy about that, because it means our team is back on track in a big way. NBA Finals, here we come!

But it is time to keep my vow, the one I put into writing on January 5. That's the trouble with journals. Written vows are, well, written down.

I will confess the truth any day now.

Love,

Penny

TUESDAY, JANUARY 13, 2015

Dear You,

Our class has been discussing Reverend Martin Luther King Jr. every day. MLK (that's what we call him) led huge marches and had a dream for African American civil rights in the 1960s. He believed in using nonviolence and love to achieve his goals.

MLK: "The time is always right to do what's right."

He was such a good man.

Sometimes, I wish with all my heart that MLK could know that we have our first African American President, Barack Obama, now. MLK would be mighty FLABBERGASTED.

Here is a flabbergasted, joyful MLK meeting President Barack Obama:

I am guessing Martin Luther King wouldn't approve of fabrications and stealing someone's precious heritage.

Of course, MLK would have advised Fabricator PVB to tell the truth.

SO THAT'S WHAT I'M GOING TO DO!!!!!!!!!!!!! TWO AND A HALF MONTHS OF FABRICATING IS LONG ENOUGH!!!

Tomorrow or the next day for sure.

Your older sib,

Penny

Another win tonight, 1/13/15. We beat the Utah Jazz, 116–105.

Another win Wednesday, 1/14. Beat Miami, 104–89.

Dear You,

I couldn't do it.

What happened was this:

On Thursday night, I was thinking about the beautiful Ohlone basket, so I drew it on a piece of cardboard, just as Great-Grandma Grace had described it. It was the best drawing I'd ever made, and I was EXCEEDINGLY proud of it. I think my professional-quality pencils made a huge difference! Unfortunately, my artwork can't be reproduced in this journal to do it justice, and it is too big to paste in.

I'm sure Hazel Pepper could have drawn everything better than I did, but I still thought it was beautiful. I also used a glitter pen, twigs, Play-Doh, and two wren feathers. Then I got carried away a bit and drew some other things, too.

Of course, I was planning to confess the truth about my fabrication right after I showed Mr. Chen my beautiful artwork yesterday.

But then Mr. Chen went BONKERS over my basket.

"Penelope! This basket is lovely! And it belongs to your family?"

"Uh, yes," I blurted out. I left out the part about it being inside Great-Grandma Grace's head.

Mr. Chen: "How extraordinary! I didn't think any Ohlone baskets existed here. I thought they'd all been taken from the Ohlone and brought back to Britain and Russia by early explorers. This should be in our Oakland museum! There is a gorgeous basket there now, but it is a replica."

My stomach went LURCHITY-LURCH. I didn't want Mr. Chen contacting Great-Grandma Grace to tell her to take her nonexistent basket to a museum, so I blurted out, "Yes, the basket is on its way to the Oakland Museum ASAP!"

Mr. Chen: "Oh, wow!"

He was actually speechless for one whole minute, staring at my drawing. All of a sudden, I felt proud of that basket, even though it wasn't really part of my own heritage.

But then I noticed he was also examining the other stuff I had done.

Mr. Chen: "It looks like you had some fun working on this."

He said he loved the details and the glitter and how I'd filled everything with a "swath" of color using my colored pencils. He also liked the "3-D effects," such as the beautiful tissue-paper ocean, colored sea-green with Magic Marker; the wren feathers in the Indian chief's headdress; and the real sticks for the teepees.

Mr. Chen: "What are those black marks at the top? Storm clouds?" They were supposed to be bison stampeding in the distance, but I knew they didn't really look like bison. Now I wasn't even sure if the Ohlone ever met up with bison. So I said, yes, that's what they were. Storm clouds.

Mr. Chen: "I think you need to rethink that headdress and, also, the tepees. You've got this tropical green thing going on. There's none of that in Northern California. There were marshes and wetlands and groves of oaks. And you've drawn too much warfare. All those spears! You may have forgotten some of what you learned about the Ohlone in third grade. And, most important of all, information about your own heritage."

Me: "Third grade was a long time ago."

I hadn't been listening that hard then either, I guess.

Then, all of a sudden, he excused himself and said he would be back in a jiffy.

Could he tell I was fabricating??????? Was he off to get the PRINCIPAL?

My hands got all sweaty. And my stomach did that LURCHITY-LURCH thing again.

Then Mr. Chen rushed back into the classroom carrying a few books he'd borrowed from Mrs. Rodriguez, one of the third-grade teachers.

Mr. Chen: "I think you will find these useful. Maybe you've read some of them already, but you should look at them again. You need to do more research."

Mr. Chen loves research.

So I admitted that I had actually used my imagination quite a bit, and I also got some information from a few old movies to make my artwork fancy-schmancy. And that it was easier to draw palm trees than oak trees.

Mr. Chen: "That's the danger of getting our history from the movies."

Me: "Also, I know the teepees aren't right, but it was fun gluing on those twigs."

He asked if I'd shown my work to my parents. I said, "Oh, yes, we discuss the Ohlone all the time," even though they hadn't seen this artwork.

Mr. Chen: "They will be interested. And you will be surprised what information you acquire from interviewing the people in your family. That's the beauty of this project—firsthand accounts, memories, and stories."

Me: "Oh, right."

Mr. Chen: "I'm sure you will glean a lot from the interview part of the project."

"I will see what I can glean," I said.

I like the word GLEAN.

I asked Mr. Chen if my beautiful artwork could take the place of the paragraph I was supposed to hand in, because a picture says a thousand words. He said, in this case, yes. But he was looking forward to words from me, too, later on.

Of course, at this point, the story and the minor fabrication involve you, since you are a part of my family and I'm your older sibling. I feel bad because you are just an innocent fetus bystander. When you get to Pacific Beach Elementary School, I hope people won't know you as THE FABRICATOR'S SIBLING. That sounds like a horror movie.

Yours,

Penny Liar Pants on Fire

A loss to Oklahoma City last night, 115–127, Friday, 1/16.

Tonight we beat Houston, 131–106.

SUNDAY, JANUARY 18, 2015

Dear You,

We are learning about METAPHORS in class. Sometimes, words paint a picture by comparing one thing to something else. But it's not always a pretty picture, You.

Here's me, spinning a WEB of lies.

And here I am digging a HOLE for myself.

Too late to climb back up. And the hole is deep. So I guess the only thing to do is try to make it a very, very interesting hole.

I have begun reading some of the books Mr. Chen lent me.

And tonight, I read something very cool.

THE OHLONE INVENTED BASKETBALL!

They liked to throw spears through a hoop. That's not exactly basketball, but it's close. The Ohlone really loved games. Racing games, games with sticks and pucks, and games throwing dice. It made them feel better after a tough hunting season. Their teams were mostly cheerful, and winners didn't brag.

The Ohlone made their home in California for thousands and thousands of years before the Europeans came. They have lived here longer than anybody. The Chochenyo, the Ohlone who lived on the eastern side of the San Francisco Bay, are Sammy's ancestors.

I close my eyes and try to imagine THOUSANDS AND THOUSANDS OF YEARS. I get slightly dizzy thinking about how long that is.

First, the Ohlone spent their time hunting small animals and gathering seeds and nuts. But when the bow and arrow were invented, they didn't have to use spears anymore. Then they could hunt bigger animals, such as deer, antelope, and large birds.

But I keep thinking about those bodies under the mall.

And so I have decided that I will make my presentation extremely interesting and informative about the Ohlone past, but I also vow to educate my classmates about the desecration of the Ohlone sacred burial sites in this modern day and age!

Love,

Penny

MONDAY, JANUARY 19, 2015

Dear You,

It is a long weekend because we have today off from school for Martin Luther King Jr. Day.

Mama and Sammy and I volunteered to get rid of invasive weeds and trash at the Martin Luther King Jr. Shoreline Park in his honor. INVASIVE means "taking over." Ugly weeds with ugly names to match (STAR THISTLE! STINKWORT!) grow where native plants have died during our drought.

Here is a drawing of MLK meeting PVB. You can't really tell from my drawing, but I am making my vow to educate my classmates about the desecration of the Ohlone sacred burial sites in this modern day and age.

Love,

Pen

FRIDAY, JANUARY 23, 2015

Dear You,

"Hey, Happy Draymond Green Day!" Hazel said when she saw us in the schoolyard this morning.

Me, privately to Gabby: "How come you told Hazel Pepper about our special Dubs greeting?"

Gabby: "How come you always call her Hazel Pepper instead of just plain Hazel?"

Me: "I do? Maybe because it's fun to say?"

Gabby: "Hmmf. Maybe you just want her to be 'Hazel Pepper, the new girl' forever?"

Yes, Feet, Gabby can READ MY MIND.

She's right. Hazel Drop-the-Pepper isn't so new anymore. She's one of us. I do not feel merry about that.

Good news, though: We beat the Houston Rockets on Wednesday, 126–113. The two teams really don't like each other. Gabby said Mike said the Houston coach doesn't think the Dubs are that good. Well, we sure showed him!

Love,

Penny

We beat the Sacramento Kings tonight, 126–101. Klay Thompson scored thirty-seven points in the third quarter! AN NBA RECORD!!!!

MONDAY, JANUARY 26, 2015

Dear You,

Mama snores at night lately. Maybe it's because she's pregnant, or maybe it's because we are having the driest January in Oakland on record, according to Mr. Chen. I hope her snoring doesn't keep you up, You. I want you to be as healthy as can be. So hold on, hold on.

Love,
Penny

PS. Dubs beat the Boston Celtics last night, 114–111. Gabby said that Mike said they could have won by much more but they didn't have the legs. They were tired from ALL THEIR WINS!

But YOUR legs are growing!

Chicago beat us 111–113, 1/27/15. Andrew Bogut had the flu and didn't play.

FRIDAY, JANUARY 30, 2015

Dear You,

Today, we didn't have school again. It was a Professional Development Day. I suppose that's an extra day for teachers to hone their skills. HONE means improve. But Mr. Chen's skills are fine just the way they are. They don't need honing.

Yesterday, he wore his Punctuation Tie.

Even when he teaches us about punctuation, it is fun. He likes to remind us that "Let's eat Grandma" is different from "Let's eat, [COMMA] Grandma!!!!!!!!!" He also says I am the Queen of Punctuation Marks, and so he always crosses out most of mine with his red pen when I use too many!!!!!!!

Gabby is interviewing her mother today about her childhood in Jamaica. I suppose I could conduct an interview with Sammy, but the trouble with Sammy is that she is so, so wise, I'm afraid she will glean that I'm fabricating.

I feel a bit sick thinking about it.

Dubs lost again tonight, to the Jazz. 100–110. Bo-gut played, but not too well. I guess he's still not feel-ing better.

Maybe I feel sick myself because of the basketball losses.

Anyway, HAPPY STEPH CURRY DAY to all.

Love,

Pen

SATURDAY, JANUARY 31, 2015

Dear You,

Dubs won against the Phoenix Suns tonight, 106–87, but I still feel sick.

Love,

Penny

SUNDAY, FEBRUARY 1, 2015

Dear You,

You are the size of a peach and about three inches long. You are now working on your vocal cords, which are useful for crying. Unfortunately, no one will hear you. That worries me a lot. I can't stop thinking about that.

That is all I can write. I have the flu.

Love,

Penny

MONDAY, FEBRUARY 2, 2015

Dear You,

I didn't go to school today. Gabby phoned to see how I was. She was impressed by my fever: 101.4. She said it sounds like a radio station.

Gabby told me "a very special thing about Hazel." Those were her exact words. Hazel Drop-the-Pepper told Gabby she has a GOAT in her backyard.

Actually, that IS kind of special. I've seen cats and dogs and chickens in backyards in my neighborhood. Sometimes even a wild turkey or a hungry deer.

Goats, hardly ever.

This is a goat:

Disregard the above goat. I won't bother erasing it,

but as you can see, it's hard for me to replicate. My professional-quality pencils aren't helping with goats.

I can't draw like Hazel, but I know words such as REPLICATE, which Hazel probably doesn't know, and I feel good about that.

I just read what I wrote to you above, Feet. If you said I sounded like a person with a heart full of envy and darkness, not love and light, you would be right. It's probably because of the flu.

I read that the Ohlone people were afraid of envy. They thought it was dangerous. So they acted kindly to one another, sharing sage and mustard seeds after harvesting their seed meadow, for instance.

Is my envy dangerous?

Love,

Pen

PS. I never did get around to interviewing Sammy. I didn't even feel like having Sundae Monday today. A very Blue Monday. I was even wearing blue pj's.

> Tuesday, 2/3/15, we beat
> Sacramento, 121–96.
> Wednesday, 2/4/15, we beat
> Dallas, 128–114.

Dear You,

I had the flu all week. But I feel much better.

Mama and Sammy prescribed Magic Tea (honey, warm water, lemon, and cayenne pepper) and rice pudding and lots of rest. I will be returning to school on Monday.

Today, Gabby came for a visit. We talked about the Warriors's wins on Tuesday and Wednesday, but mostly about last night's loss to the Atlanta Hawks, 116–124. It was an important game between the two teams with the best records in the NBA this year.

Gabby said Hazel Drop-the-Pepper told her she's not worried about that loss. Well, Gabby and I agree that she should be! VERY worried! Atlanta looked pretty good to us true Warriors fans.

It felt great to be with a Dubs fan who understands that every game counts!

Gabby brought me a Get Well card from Hazel Drop-the-Pepper, and wasn't that kind of her?

I guess so, but big deal.

Gabby stayed to watch the game. We felt better because the Dubs beat the Knicks, 106–92! Gabby said that Mike said that Steve Kerr almost decided to coach the Knicks before he decided to coach the Warriors. I'll bet Coach Kerr is happy he chose OUR TEAM!

I guess it's time to glean stuff from Sammy in an interview, now that I'm feeling better.

By the way, *What to Expect When You're Expecting* says you may have the beginning of a little hairdo. You are the size of a clenched fist.

Love,

Penny

MONDAY, FEBRUARY 9, 2015

Dear You,

I had a BIG scare today! I completely forgot about OPEN HOUSE night at school, but Mama and Sammy didn't. They note every single thing down in their iPhones. I was sure Mama and Sammy would find out about the project from Mr. Chen!

Uncle Ziggy stayed home with me to watch the game. He kept asking me why I was so quiet and pale. I said I was still recuperating from the flu.

But Mr. Chen revealed nothing about the project to Mama and Sammy. He did say he was happy to have me in the class and that I am an enthusiastic learner.

Whew!

So no Monday blues tonight. Warriors beat Phila-
delphia, 89–84!

And I got to taste Mint-Pistachio for Sundae Monday, since I was too sick last Monday. Pretty good, but
not as good as Rum Raisin.

Love,

Pen

TUESDAY, FEBRUARY 10, 2015

Dear You,

I got another scare tonight when Sammy asked:
"What's all this about your interest in the Ohlone?"

LURCH!

But it was Grandma Lorraine who had told them
about my curiosity.

Mama: "Is this something you had to do for school?"

Me, thinking quickly: "No, no, I just like California
history. We are learning about American Indian soci-
eties, but I want to make sure I glean all about YOUR
heritage, Sammy. And I love doing research, just like
both of you do when you are working on websites and
history lectures."

Sammy: "A history buff like your mama! How

great that you are broadening your interests beyond basketball."

Mama went straight to her little kitchen desk and came back holding a notebook with a French poodle on its cover.

Mama: "For your research."

I guess she had bought a discount pack of dog notebooks and had not given me the golden retriever one because they were planning to get me a golden retriever, as I'd hoped.

Me, casual as can be: "So, anyway, I'm curious. What does your Ohlone heritage mean to you?"

Sammy: "My heritage?"

She furrowed her brow, really thinking hard about my question.

Sammy: "Well, I have two heritages, as you know. My German heritage and my Ohlone heritage. My German ancestors came here a hundred years ago. And the California Ohlone have lived here just about forever!"

Sammy was looking all starry-eyed and proud, thinking about her heritage and her many tangled-up roots. But then she said, "It is my Ohlone heritage that has a bigger part of my heart. I guess you cherish something more when it's in danger of being erased."

So I told Mama and Sammy what I had learned from Grandma Lorraine and Great-Grandma Grace. About the shell mound being destroyed and the mall built on top of the sacred burial spot and all those forgotten bodies discovered by the construction workers.

Mama and Sammy glanced at each other.

Mama: "They told you about that? We've been trying to protect you from that sad story. But I guess you're old enough to know."

You will learn pretty quickly, You. Parents can be OVERprotective. Of course I'm old enough!

Sammy: "Here's the important thing to remember, Penny. The Ohlone didn't disappear. We're not just descriptions in old books. We're not just names on streets and parks. A long time ago, people took our land. They made us live in the California missions. They tried to force us to forget our language and our customs and our stories. They disrespected our dead. But guess what? We're still here!"

Me: "We sure are!"

Sammy didn't hear that, I don't think.

Meanwhile, Mama was looking down at her fingernails, probably feeling sad about being an orphan. Sometimes, I want to see Mama all starry-eyed about her family tree, too.

Anyway, I have lots to write about in the interview section of my project now.

Love,

Penny

WEDNESDAY, FEBRUARY 11, 2015

Happy Klay Thompson Day to all.

We beat the Timberwolves, 94–91. Everybody thinks the score was too close for comfort.

Hazel-Drop-the-Pepper gave me a friendly thumbs-up today, and said "Hey, go Dubs!" She is trying very hard to be my friend.

By the way, Hazel Drop-the-Pepper's thumbs are double-jointed. So her thumbs-up is really a "thumbs-upside-down." She demonstrated to some kids the other day and they were all impressed. I guess I was, too. Hazel can bend the top half of each thumb backward.

Love,
Penny

SATURDAY, FEBRUARY 14, 2015

Dear You,

It is Valentine's Day.

On this day, people send cards and give gifts to show those in their lives how much they love them, in case they haven't told them on other days of the year.

Mama and Sammy think Valentine's Day is unnecessary. That's because we all know how we feel about one another already.

They also think Valentine's Day is too commercial, just a day for businesses to try to get people to spend their money. They don't believe in purchasing cards for Valentine's Day. So we mostly exchange homemade ones. But last year, Uncle Ziggy brought over a big box of store-bought candy for us. This year, he brought daffodils from his garden.

True confession to you, You: I was hoping for store-bought candy, especially the chocolate-covered cherries and the lemon drops with caramel centers. I didn't want to hurt Uncle Ziggy's feelings, so I didn't say anything.

Anyway, love must be extremely complicated, because we humans sing about it a lot. If you took a count of all the songs sung on 99.7 or even 106.1, my favorite radio stations, they are mostly love songs.

Hazel Drop-the-Pepper disagrees: "No, most songs are about money. And that's what my mom and her boyfriend mostly argue about, even though they are madly, truly, deeply in love."

Gabby: "I'd say probably even between love and money."

We'll have to test our song theories one day.

In the schoolyard yesterday, Gabby and I started singing that song everyone knows, about the world needing more love-sweet-love, because there's just too little of it, sometimes.

And, of course, Hazel Drop-the-Pepper had to join in and wreck our almost-perfect harmony. And then Kenny heard us, and he sang:

What the world needs now is BOOGERS, sweet boogers.
It's the only thing there's just too little of.

He is so, so immature. I hope I don't think of his verse every time I sing that song.

Anyway, Love-Sweet-Love to you, too.

Penny

PS. I was also hoping there would be a proposal of marriage in our house today. The proposer wouldn't have to get all that commercial about it with roses or champagne or a diamond ring, etcetera. Just a simple Valentine's Day marriage proposal would have been very romantic. But that didn't happen.

LATER, SAME NIGHT

I have decided that in honor of Valentine's Day, I will now tell you the name of my secret impossible love:

Gabby's older brother.

My heart flutters when I think about Mike and his musical voice.

BE STILL, MY HEART. I read that somewhere, but I forget where.

I know he is six years older than I am, but even

if he was a fifth grader, I am positive he would not be immature. And six years won't make as much of a difference when we are older. I am too shy to tell Gabby that I like her brother, even though I have always told her everything. So I am telling you, You.

By the way, I am very glad to read in *What to Expect* that (1) your ears have moved from your neck to the sides of your head and (2) your eyes have moved from the sides of your head to the front of your face. Don't get me wrong. Looks aren't everything.

Still.

Love,

Penny

WEDNESDAY, FEBRUARY 18, 2015

Dear You,

On Monday, school was closed for Presidents' Day.

So Gabby invited Hazel Drop-the-Pepper and me to a sleepover Sunday night.

Gabby's parents had a dose of bad luck after they chose names for their three kids. Two-thirds of their offspring, a whole 67 percent, were given names that don't fit. Gabby is not gabby. She has Quiet Confidence like her brother, Mike. Their little five-year-old sister's name is Angel. Unfortunately, Angel turned out to be a pest.

And Mike is just Mike. I looked up Michael in Mama and Sammy's book *One Thousand and One Names for Baby*, and Michael is one of the archangels in the Bible. So Mike is an angel, not Angel. At least their parents got one name right.

Anyway, when Gabby's friends are over, Angel sleeps in their parents' bedroom on an air bed. But this time, Angel wanted to have a sleepover with "the big girls," and her parents said she could. So there were four of us in the room. Angel had the bottom bunk all to herself and Gabby was in the top bunk. Hazel Drop-the-Pepper and I were in sleeping bags on the floor.

Part of me thinks that Angel has a right to sleep in her own bed, but a big part of me thinks she is a pest. She kept blowing raspberries and making farting noises so we'd pay attention to her.

At sleepovers, we usually end up talking about all sorts of things in the dark (the Dubs, of course, and boys, etcetera, etcetera).

Then, all of a sudden, Gabby changed the subject and started blabbing about you, You! I had told Gabby that you weren't a secret anymore, but I didn't think she'd bring you up so soon, especially in front of Hazel Drop-the-Pepper!

Gabby: "Penny's mama is having a baby."

Hazel: "Really? Oh, that's great!"

Gabby: "Hey, I have a question, Penny. Where did this baby happen to come from?"

I have been waiting for Gabby to ask this question. I knew it must be inside of her, like a caramel center you know is there, hiding inside a lemon drop.

Hazel: "What do you mean? Don't you know where babies come from? Don't you know the Facts of Life?"

Gabby: "Of course I know the Facts of Life!"

Hazel: "Then if you know the Facts of Life, you know where Penny's mom's baby came from!"

Gabby: "I just told you. I DO know the Facts of Life! But I was wondering because, you know, Penny has two moms."

Hazel: "Penny has two moms?"

All of a sudden, Angel piped up. She had stopped making her noises, and we'd figured she was asleep. But no, she had been listening, and she wanted to know what the Facts of Life were. Nobody said anything at first. We didn't know how to explain those Facts to a five-year-old.

Then Gabby said, "They're nothing. Go to sleep."

Hazel: "The Facts of Life are things we learn and things we know." And I guess that was the right answer for Angel.

Angel: "I know a fact. Red paint and yellow paint mixed together make orange paint."

We tried not to laugh. We didn't want to hurt Angel's feelings, even though she is a pest. Of course, a few giggle snorts did bubble out. But it was OK, because Angel laughed, too, even though she didn't really know what we were all laughing at.

I was glad that Gabby and Hazel Drop-the-Pepper fell asleep before they could ask me any more questions about the Facts of Life. It felt too personal to talk about private things in front of a stranger. Hazel Drop-the-Pepper isn't a stranger, exactly. But still.

You, I just want to say right now that you are a Fact of Life.

A fifteen-and-a-half-week, miraculous, wonderful one. And I love you a lot already.

Love,
Penny

Warriors beat the San Antonio
Spurs on Friday, 2/20/15, 110–99.

A loss to the Pacers on Sunday,
2/22/15, 98–104.

We beat the Washington Wizards
on Tuesday, 2/24/15, 114–107.

THURSDAY, FEBRUARY 26, 2015

Dear You,

You win some, you lose some.

That's what Gabby said. Her voice went deeper and her eyes got all squinty, and that meant she was quoting Mike, as usual. I almost told her I liked him, but I was much too shy.

I'm DIZZY! We win, then we lose, then we win, then we lose again. We lost to the Cavaliers to-night, 99–110.

Mama says winning and losing are parts of life. I will try to remember that as your older sibling, You.

But it's hard.

By the way, we all hate the Cavs' LeBron James with a passion!

Not just because he is a good player on an opposing team, although that's part of the reason. We hate him because he is a TRAITOR. That means a person who has betrayed someone. A while ago, LeBron James left his home team, the Cleveland Cavaliers, to join the Miami Heat. Fans in Cleveland were absolutely HEARTBROKEN! Now he is back with Cleveland, but lots of people can't forgive him, even if it's all in the past.

I can't even imagine Steph Curry doing that to Oakland fans!

I was watching the game with Gabby and Mike at their house. They have a colossal TV. Mike said the colossal screen makes LeBron's head look more conceited than ever. Mike makes me laugh.

Love,

Me

FRIDAY, FEBRUARY 27, 2015

Dear You,

What to Expect says you are moving your arms and

legs, but Mama says she doesn't feel anything yet.

And you are practicing your sucking and swallowing, getting set for the real world of eating and drinking, when you are finally free from the umbilical cord attaching you to all of Mama's chewed-up meals.

By the way, the Splash Brothers are back! Dubs beat the Raptors tonight, 113–89. I feel sorry for Toronto because they lost four games in a row, but still.

Today, Mr. Chen said our written interviews with our families were interesting. His eyes beamed sparkles at me. I felt glad and guilty at the same time. That is a very strange feeling.

Love,

Pen

SATURDAY, FEBRUARY 28, 2015

Dear You,

I forgot to tell you that yesterday Gabby and I were both wishing we had a basketball coach and a team to play for, and then WE READ EACH OTHER'S MINDS!

"Mike!" we said at the very same time.

My heart fluttered.

Gabby is going to ask him to be our coach. But

meanwhile, we got permission to post a sign-up sheet for girl players on the bulletin board outside the school office. We want to get enough sign-ups for a team at first, but maybe we'll get enough for a whole league!

xxx,

Pen

SUNDAY, MARCH 1, 2015

Dear You,

Hazel Drop-the-Pepper is a "latchkey kid." That's what she calls herself. She has a key to her house pinned inside her backpack. Her mom, Liza, and her mom's live-in boyfriend, Rick, come home after dark. Today they went on a date which lasted all day and evening. So Hazel often has to let herself in.

Tonight, Hazel Drop-the-Pepper stayed for dinner because she told Sammy the pot roast smelled delicious and she could smell it all the way from our front yard. So of course she got an invitation after saying that.

Uncle Ziggy was over, too. He was in a celebratory mood because he will be starting a computer course tomorrow. He is going to help Sammy with her web design business, which is growing. He won't have to show his resume to Sammy. She already knows what he's like. And he could still be a troubadour when they take breaks from work.

He was also in a celebratory mood because he had just received a tip about another secret stairway. He couldn't share the information because he hasn't checked it out, and it's still a secret.

Then Hazel Drop-the-Pepper said an amazing thing. She said she has a secret stairway almost right next door to her house, not far from us! Uncle Ziggy was flabbergasted! His secret stairway group didn't know about that one, but Hazel said, oh, yesiree, it's there all right.

I will believe it when I see it.

Here is a confession, You:

I have a terrible niggling suspicion about Hazel Drop-the-Pepper.

I THINK SHE IS A FABRICATOR AS WELL AS A BRAGGART!

I admit that I, too, am a fabricator. Maybe it takes one fabricator to sniff out another fabricator.

HAZEL DROP-THE-PEPPER'S POSSIBLE FABRICATIONS:

Her gigantic bedroom. She says that wherever they live, her mom always lets Hazel have the master bedroom all to herself.

A refrigerator in that room!

The secret stairway.

That goat, of course.

And it also seems to me that every time someone brings up something, Hazel Drop-the-Pepper can match it. Better than match it. I tested that theory a couple of times.

Me: "Our family may take a summer trip to Disneyland."

Hazel: "Ours, too! I've been lots of times, but there is always something new to see."

Me: "My mother and Sammy may get married one day, I think."

Hazel: "Rick and my mother are getting married for sure. VERY soon! Probably any day now."

Me: "Mama and Sammy bought an old butter churner in an antique shop in Sonoma. They use it for an umbrella stand, but they may try to bring it on *Antiques Roadshow*."

Hazel: "We have an old samovar that used to belong to a Russian czar's cousin. We think it's worth thousands."

Me: "Sammy has a friend in the California State Assembly."

Hazel: "Rick, my mother's boyfriend, has a best friend

in the Senate. In Washington! He has so many important friends! Including Steve Kerr, coach of the Warriors!"

Hmmm . . . See what I mean?

Hazel Drop-the-Pepper phoned her mom and got permission to stay for the game, too.

Another win! We beat the Celtics, 106–101. At one point in the middle of the second quarter, the Dubs were behind by twenty-six points, but Hazel said it probably felt like only two points to the Celtics.

Hazel: "That's how good the Dubs are. Don't worry. The Dubs will catch up."

Later, Uncle Ziggy said Hazel Drop-the-Pepper knows a lot about basketball for a young person.

I guess.

Hazel's mother, Liza, came to pick her up after we watched the game. She looks like Hazel but much skinnier, with the same big off-and-on smile.

Love,

Penny

MONDAY, MARCH 2, 2015

Dear You,

I told Mama and Sammy that I felt like I had been having a HEART ATTACK during the game tonight against the Nets. Mama told me not to joke about things like that. Well, my heart WAS pounding, hard. Then I remembered that Sammy's dad, Henry Bach, had died of a heart attack, so I apologized. Sammy told Mama not to be so hard on me.

But in my own defense, it was one of the most exciting games ever!

Even Mama and Sammy watched the exciting finish. (Well, exciting, but SAD. For our team.) The Dubs were down ten points in the fourth. Curry made FOUR three-pointers, bringing the Warriors back, but then the Nets' Jarrett Jack made a jumper AT THE LAST SECOND, and the Dubs lost 108–110.

I feel bad for being insensitive to the memory of Henry Bach. But still.

NEWS: Hazel Drop-the-Pepper invited Gabby and me over to her house tomorrow. I am looking forward to going.

She wouldn't invite us to her house if she was a guilty fabricator, would she? So I feel a bit bad about MALIGNING her, even if I was only accusing her in this journal.

Do you look forward to anything, You?

I guess not. "Looking forward" means you can think. But I do like to imagine that you can think!

Sometimes, I have so many thoughts in my head, I am not sure what to do with them all. That's why I like to write my thoughts down.

And *What to Expect* says you can yawn now that you are entering your eighteenth week. Do you ever get bored and yawn into the darkness? You can also hiccup.

Love,

Penny

PS. Somebody scribbled SASHA OBAMA, the name of one of President Obama's daughters, on our basketball list on the bulletin board at school. A prank, of course. Ha ha. There were no other new names.

PPS. Strawberry-Mint for Sundae Monday, all month. Pretty good.

TUESDAY, MARCH 3, 2015

Dear You,

As I told you, the Ohlone were excellent hunters. Their senses were highly attuned to the natural world because their survival depended on it. AMAZING FACT: They could sometimes smell an animal even before they could see it. That's how keen their senses were trained to be.

Here's the thing, You. Human beings have five senses. Taste, smell, sight, hearing, and touch. I am not sure about the order in which you will develop them.

Do you have a sense of smell yet?

WHAT I LOVE TO SMELL
Mama's weekend French toast with vanilla
Roses
Coffee in the kitchen when Sammy's working late
Shampoo in the shower
Rain and its clean, pine-needle scent
Love,
Penny

PS. PRINCESS LEIA was on the basketball list. Same handwriting as SASHA OBAMA. So immature.

Wednesday, 3/4/15, we beat the Bucks, 102–93. Curry made three three-pointers in one minute in the fourth quarter!

HAPPY BIRTHDAY, Draymond Green! And thank you for the twenty-three points!

SATURDAY, MARCH 7, 2015

Dear You,

> A double-digit win last night,
> 3/6/15, against Dallas, 104–89!

Everything Hazel said about herself checked out. No fabrications. I am relieved, actually. I suppose I am beginning to like her a little bit.

Hazel's bedroom is the biggest kid's bedroom I've ever seen. She has giant posters of Dubs players on every wall and a practice net on her closet door. She has a four-poster bed and a rocking chair and a window seat, AND—

A REFRIGERATOR.

Check!

Yes, her very own refrigerator! There is only a carton of lemonade in it right now, but Hazel said she usually keeps apples and beef jerky in there for snacking.

Her refrigerator makes a nice humming noise that lulls her to sleep when she is having trouble with that.

SAMOVAR

Check!

A samovar is a big, old-fashioned brass object that people used to make tea, especially in Russia. Hazel's mother made a lamp base out of theirs. I didn't get around to asking if it once belonged to a czar's cousin.

Here is what it looks like, sort of:

GOAT
Check!

Yes, Hazel has a goat in her backyard!!!!!

Her name is Nell and she's two years old. She is very big and soft and warm and brown with long floppy ears and kind eyes. A Nubian goat, Hazel says.

And we all got to milk her!!! Hazel's mom tied her legs to the milking stand so she wouldn't kick, and her head stuck through bars on a stock like this:

Nell chomped happily on her alfalfa while we milked her. It was hard to aim the stream of milk into the pail, and we got goat's milk on our clothes. We didn't care! We even tasted the milk with our fingers. It was warm and sweet.

Goats are very stubborn, Hazel said. They don't do what you want them to do most of the time. But we took turns getting her to follow us by holding small amounts of grain in our palms. Nubian goats go crazy for grain.

Sometimes, Nell hollers "M-AH-AH-AH-AH!!" Especially when she is out of food. She has spectacular vocal cords.

Not too long ago, neighbors called the fire department because they thought they'd heard a crying child. Everyone got a good laugh out of that.

Except Hazel's mom's boyfriend, Rick. He didn't think it was a laughing matter. He is not a goat lover, Hazel says.

Hazel says Nell is both smart and not-so-smart. Sometimes, she poops in her drinking water. But Nell knows things. For instance, she only nuzzles the hair of a person who really loves her, no matter what. Hazel whispers secrets to her, and Nell whispers secrets back. Hazel swears she does.

THE SECRET STAIRWAY

Check!

You walk four steps down an alley, and there it is. Seven stone steps going up, easy to miss because of a neighbor's trash cans in front of the alley's entrance. It's the trash cans that keep the stairway secret. Maybe that's why the Oakland Secret Stairway Society hasn't discovered it yet.

The stairway stops at another neighbor's old rickety fence—for absolutely no reason. Once, Hazel peeked over that fence, standing on a little stool she'd carried up the stairs. She was hoping to see a beautiful secret garden or something intriguing and mysterious, like an elf's house. But all she saw was some straggly grass and a swing set. Nothing intriguing at all.

Hazel: "But it's still a secret stairway, and we are the only ones who know about it. An IRONCLAD secret!"

(I admire Hazel for using that word. It is a wonderful word.)

Gabby: "Maybe it is a stairway where we TELL secrets."

Hazel and I: "Yes!"

Hazel: "Let's start with boys."

TO BE CONTINUED AFTER DINNER . . .

LATER

So, PRESENTING:

SECRETS OF THE SECRET STAIRWAY (SOSS)
FIRST EDITION

GABBY'S SECRET:
Gabby has a crush on a boy named Bo in the other fifth-grade class. She has liked him since third grade, when he always shared his fruit rolls. She's not sure she likes him as much as she did in third grade, though.

She had another secret. Her brother, Mike, is taking his driver's license test soon, and she hopes he doesn't pass the test right away.

She feels so mean and guilty to even THINK that.

But when he's a driver, he won't be home as much. She will miss him.

I told Gabby that Sammy says worrying about something doesn't mean it will happen. Maybe Mike won't be gone more. We agreed that Sammy is very wise and we hope she is right.

Because where would Mike go? I wonder. He is only sixteen and can't go on long road trips or anything.

MY SECRET:

I said that I had a secret love, but I wanted to keep it private for now. I asked them to respect that. They agreed to, because that's what friends are for.

Then I also confessed that I keep wishing Mama and Sammy would get married in the near future, even though they already have a marriage of the heart.

Gabby said, yes, they should get married, because a wedding is worth it for the hors d'oeuvres. That's something the French invented, and Gabby says it's pronounced "or derves" not "horse doo-vers" like I've always thought. Her aunty Lue is a caterer, and that's what they serve at fancy-schmancy catered occasions—teeny, yummy hot and cold things that are very expensive. Shrimp balls. Tiny tacos. Spring rolls. Radish roses. Teeny quiches. Yum! You can walk around and choose seconds and thirds from people carrying the hors d'oeuvres piled up on platters. Imagine that! Gabby had them at her cousin's wedding, and she says they were the best things she ever ate in her life.

She is thinking about being a caterer herself. You probably get to eat all the leftovers. (Gabby is always thinking about what she wants to be as an adult. She thinks about that a lot. I never do. Does that mean Gabby is more mature than I am?)

Anyway, hors d'oeuvres aren't why I want Mama and Sammy to get married, of course.

I don't know why I do. I just do.

HAZEL'S SECRET:

It's an AMAZING one!!!

Hazel: "As you know, Rick is a friend of Warriors coach Steve Kerr and other important people. He is going to get great Warriors tickets for me and my mom and himself, as well as some friends of my choosing, who will be—TA-DA!—the two of you! We will probably sit near the Warriors' bench. I wasn't going to say anything until it happens, but I can't help it!!!"

Gabby and I started hooting and hollering, then we quieted down because, after all, it's a secret stairway.

Still, WOW.

Then Hazel said: "I don't like any boy at the moment, secret or not secret. But Penny, if you can't tell us the name of your secret love, can you tell us if it's a girl or a boy?"

Me: "It's a boy."

Hazel: "I'm surprised."

Me: "Why?"

Hazel: "Well, you know."

Me: "Because I have two moms?"

Hazel: "Right."

Me: "Parents don't teach you who to love, silly! Your own heart teaches you, usually by fluttering. You just love whom you love."

Mama and Sammy are always telling me that. And now I know they are right.

Hazel: "Really?"

Me: "Really."

Sometimes, I feel wiser than other kids my age.

By the way, nobody asked again about the Fact of Your Life, You.

But I think I am ready for when they do.

Love,

P

SUNDAY, MARCH 8, 2015

Dear You,

BIG NEWS!

No, not that we had a bit of rain this week. (Good news, but not the Big News.)

And not that Rick got those Warriors tickets. Not yet, anyway. Maybe he is waiting for the playoff season.

And not that Mike agreed to be a coach, because

he didn't. Gabby asked him, but he said he is too worried about his driver's license test lately. He promised he would give it some thought later. (I am very disappointed. But I understand his feelings, I guess.)

And not that the Warriors beat the Clippers tonight, 106–98.

(Happy news, but not the Big News.)

BIG NEWS!

MAMA FELT YOU MOVE!!!

When Curry dribbled behind his back and got through three defenders to make that first three-pointer, I was yelling my head off.

All of a sudden, Mama shouted, too: "The baby moved!"

Mama was wearing headphones and listening to music, so I don't think she was following the game.

But maybe YOU were!

It is fun to imagine that you were pumping your tiny fist at that moment. Or kicking a tiny foot. Or doing the wave (hee-hee).

"What did it feel like? What did it feel like?" Sammy and I kept asking her.

It was a very small feeling, Mama said. Like the flutter of a butterfly's wing. Or her cell phone vibrating. But, yup, it was a definite something.

You are a definite something!

Of course, we knew that already.

But maybe you are telling us that, now, Mama, Sammy, and I are definite somethings to you.

Love,

Pen

MONDAY, MARCH 9, 2015

Dear Definite Something,

We added Hazel's name to the basketball list at school. At first, we were excited because there were other names on the list.

STEPHANIE CURRY and KLAYMILLA THOMPSON and ANDREA BOGUT.

Gabby: "Look again. The same terrible handwriting as the fake Sasha Obama and Princess Leia."

Hazel said she recognized Kenny Walinhoff's handwriting, which looks like tangled-up yarn. She has a good memory for that kind of thing, because she is an artist.

Love,

Pen

The Dubs beat the Suns tonight, 3/9/15, 98–80! FIFTY

WINS and counting for the Dubs
this season!

FRIDAY, MARCH 13, 2015

Dear You,

Hazel and I watched the game at Gabby's.

We lost to the Nuggets, 104–113.

Mike watched the game with us. He sat beside me. He made me feel better about our loss. Steve Kerr didn't use his top players for this game, Mike said. He wanted to rest them up for the playoffs.

Mike always has a mature point of view.

Love,

Pen

PS. Another name on the future girls' basketball team list on the bulletin board. Gabby's neighbor was picking up her little granddaughter at school, and she suggested her other granddaughter, who goes to another school. CANDY JACKSON. A real name with a real phone number. Gabby phoned Candy and told her we are waiting for our coach to pass his driver's license test.

I have never known anyone named Candy, and

neither have Hazel or Gabby. It is an interesting holiday-celebration-birthday-party kind of name.

If you are a girl, You, maybe we will name you Candy.

Except it also makes me think of cavities and dentists. So maybe not.

I hope some more (real) girls sign up.

SATURDAY, MARCH 14, 2015

Dear You,

Today, I learned so much about the lowly acorn! It is not so lowly. It provided the Ohlone with nutritious and delicious eating. But a lot of work went into making the acorns edible. After the harvest, the women had to hull the acorns one at a time, then pound the acorn kernels into flour, all day long with mortars and pestles.

POUND! POUND! POUND! was a good sound to the Ohlone. It was the sound of home.

The acorn flour was put in special baskets so that hot water could be poured over it to leach out the bitter tannins. Then the flour was heated and cooked in another kind of basket, using hot stones.

It was made into a wonderful mush, which was probably a lot like the polenta Mama makes sometimes.

My home has cooking sounds. Sammy clanks pots when she cooks. Mama pounds bread dough.

Dubs beat the Knicks at home
tonight, 125–94.

HAPPY 27TH BIRTHDAY, STEPH!

Love,
Pen

SUNDAY, MARCH 15, 2015

Dear You,

NEWS: Mike passed his driver's license test!!!!!

I have never seen Mike so proud and happy. I am happy for him, too, and not only because now he will have time to coach us, of course. A person is always happy when the person that person loves is happy.

Gabby says her prediction about him was all wrong! He has been hanging around more than ever, jumping up from whatever he's doing, begging to drive anyone anywhere anytime in his parents' car. He is always excited to drive to Safeway or Rite Aid, even if someone needs just one thing, like a quart of milk or aspirin or paper clips. He will take anyone anywhere.

Mike: "Anyone need anything? Anyone need anything?"

He would nag Gabby to finish up her homework so they could go to Fentons for ice cream on a school night. He even paid. Then their parents put a stop to those trips.

This weekend, Mike drove us around Lake Merritt. THREE times! Oh, You! Lake Merritt is awesomely beautiful, with kayaks and sparkling little waves and happy joggers and walkers and geese on the green grass all around it. A lake right inside our city! Gabby said that three times around the lake was one or two times too many, but I thought it was romantic. I could have driven around Lake Merritt with Mike all afternoon. It was like having a boyfriend, except that Gabby and that pest Angel were with us.

Then Angel begged him to take us to Children's Fairyland. Mike said sure. He said he liked going there because it's so easy to park in the big lot.

Gabby: "Mike! Not Fairyland! Penny and I are too old for a puppet show and the little old woman who lived in a shoe!"

Me: "We sure are."

I did NOT want to go to Fairyland, because it seemed so babyish, as if Mike was our babysitter. On the other hand, I DID want to go to Fairyland because it's fun. I guess that's called being AMBIVALENT, when you want to and don't want to do something.

Angel wasn't ambivalent. She demanded that Mike take her to Fairyland that minute.

So Mike dropped us at Hazel's and said he'd pick us up after Fairyland. We said don't bother, thank you— Hazel only lives a block away from Gabby and me!

Liza, and her boyfriend, Rick, were in their living room. Rick smokes.

I read that the Ohlone smoked, too, but in this modern day and age, we know that smoking is bad for you. I don't know any other smokers. The cigarettes smell up Hazel's house.

Also, Rick is crabby.

I am going to admit something:

I really don't like Rick.

Still, I am trying to have EMPATHY. Having empathy means you can understand how another person is feeling. Smokers are addicted, and that must be hard. Maybe that's why he is so crabby.

But secondhand smoke is known to be bad for you, too. So because of the secondhand smoke, we went into the backyard to snuggle with Nell, because even goat smells are better than cigarette smells.

After that, we walked over to the Secret Stairway. We had all decided to finally have our Facts of Life conversation.

I felt ready.

I will try to record my Facts of Life conversation with Hazel and Gabby as accurately as I can. Because I know I will have pretty much the same conversation with you, You, when you are old enough.

To be continued later.

BEFORE BED

And now for another installment of:

SECRETS OF THE SECRET STAIRWAY (SOSS)
THE FACTS OF LIFE EDITION

Gabby: "I am glad we waited to have this conversation when Angel wasn't with us. She is too young to understand these things. The Facts of Life are about private, beautiful, mature things."

Me: "Yes, life and love and babies and families. Those things are more important than anything. So you have to be mature."

Hazel: "I hate when immature people laugh about the Facts of Life. The Facts are not a laughing matter."

Gabby: "You know what some people call the Facts of Life? The Story of the Birds and the Bees!"

Me: "FACT: Humans do NOT lay eggs and then sit on them to keep them warm!"

We laughed our heads off at that, but not out of immaturity, of course.

Then we became very quiet. It's Sunday, so there wasn't any noisy traffic at the bottom of the secret stairs. But the whole wide world seemed quiet, too, even the birds and the bees! We were waiting for one of us to start this very important conversation. None of us knew how to do it.

Finally, Hazel said, "OK, here are the Facts I know. When a man and a woman are in love and want to make a baby, the sperm from the father's penis enters the mother's vagina when the father puts his penis there. Then the sperm travels up to the woman's uterus to fertilize the egg that's waiting for it."

Gabby: "Those are the Facts I know, too. And also, the man and woman kiss."

Then they both looked at me, waiting for the Facts they didn't know.

Me: "So, same thing: Sperm plus Egg equals Baby. Plus kiss. But when two women are in love and want to start a family, the sperm can enter the mother's vagina using a syringe. The mothers can get the sperm from a sperm bank, where kindly men have deposited their sperm to help other people create families."

Gabby and Hazel said, "Oh." They were quiet again for a while.

Hazel: "Well, I think it's nice that all kinds of families can have babies."

Gabby: "Yes, babies are fun. Sometimes."

Of course, she was thinking about her sister, Angel, the pest.

Then Hazel asked about the father of our baby.

I explained that when you are eighteen, You, your sperm donor has agreed to meet you, if that's what you want. It will be entirely up to you.

Hazel said it's much harder for a daughter when she has known her father very, very well, ever since she was born, and then she doesn't see him much at all lately, except during summer vacation, although he had to skip last summer and she misses him terribly.

Of course, she was talking about her own dad, who lives in Cincinnati.

I felt so much empathy for Hazel then. I told Hazel that even my situation is easier than hers. I mean, having a father whom you don't remember and don't miss at all. Or maybe just a little bit. And maybe I only remember him from his photograph.

Of course, I have double the love from Mama and Sammy!

And so do you, You.

Everything is relative, right?

Love,

Pen

PS. Can't wait to take you to Fairyland.

MONDAY, MARCH 16, 2015

Dear You,

The Dubs are going to the playoffs! Only the top eight teams from the Western Conference get to go, and we are #1! And then the winner of the West plays the winner of the East for the NBA Finals.

Love,

Pen

Beat the Lakers tonight,
108–105. Klay hurt his ankle
in the third quarter!

Feel better, Klay!

TUESDAY, MARCH 17, 2015

Dear You,

Nobody likes it when her parents argue. Scary thoughts about divorce wiggle like worms into your mind. It's true that Mama and Sammy only have a marriage of the heart, but if they weren't together, it would still HURT like a divorce.

A divorce of the heart.

Sammy brought home a bunch of paint chips for your room. But Mama said Sammy's paint samples weren't necessary, because we don't need to get your room ready yet.

And soon after that, Sammy and Mama had an argument.

I must have had a worried look on my face.

Mama said to me: "What's with the hangdog expression, kiddo? This is what's known as a heated discussion, that's all."

Me: "It sounded like you were arguing."

Sammy: "OK, let's call a spade a spade and an argument an argument. What's wrong with arguing? It clears the air!"

The air really did need clearing.

The air felt like it was filled with little sharp electricity zaps straight from their thoughts. Mama and Sammy had turned those electricity zaps into words, and then it sure sounded like an argument to me.

THE ARGUMENT:

Sammy wants to find out if you are a boy or a girl before you are officially born.

Mama doesn't.

When Mama has something called an ULTRA-SOUND, a special camera on her belly, they may be able to see the baby's penis if it's a boy. Parents can choose to have the ultrasound technician give them that information. Or not.

But sometimes the penis is hidden or blurry so you don't really know if it's there.

Mama: "So if we don't see anything, we won't know anything for sure, anyway."

Sammy: "But what if we DO see something? Then we'll know."

Mama: "Why do we have to know? Don't we want it to be a surprise when the baby is born?"

Sammy slapped the palm of her hand on her forehead. That's a thing she does when she's annoyed.

Sammy: "Won't it be a surprise no matter WHEN we find out?"

And that's when Mama started to cry.

And that's when Sammy and I really, really listened to Mama and had empathy.

It turns out it's not about the surprise at all. It's about Mama being scared that something bad may happen, like it did when Mama had those other pregnancies that didn't work out. And if Mama knows whether you are a boy or a girl, then she'll have a mind-picture of you. If something bad happens to you, it will hurt more because of that mind-picture.

"Remember," Sammy said, just like she always does, "worrying about something doesn't mean it will happen." But she gave Mama a big hug. And told Mama she understood.

Mama: "What if you found out it was a girl? Would you really paint a girl's room PETUNIA PINK? Would you paint a boy's room BOBBIN' ROBIN BLUE?"

Sammy and I said "Ugh!" at the same time.

And that's when we all laughed and the argument was over.

As for me, I don't care if you are a boy or a girl, You. And I will wait until you are safely born to find out, if that's what Mama wants.

Because I just think of you as You, Precious You, right now. You are as real to me as anything, and it doesn't matter if you are a boy or a girl.

I do worry every now and then, though. Just a bit.

So hang in there, little You.

Please.

Love,

Pen

PS. I read that Ohlone babies of long ago slept in cradles, woven like baskets and decorated with beads and shells. But the Ohlone thought it was bad luck to make those cradles before their babies were born. They would have understood how Mama felt.

THURSDAY, MARCH 19, 2015

Dear You,

Things are proceeding APACE. I have always wanted to say that.

But I think *apace* is the kind of word I would feel weird saying out loud. Writing it is different.

So. Things are proceeding apace.

Mama's belly is too big for her jeans. She has to wear pants with elasticized waists.

And Mama says you are moving a bit every day.

I am struck with awe and happiness at the thought of you. Now I really understand what *awestruck* and *awesome* mean.

You will soon be a part of us. Like a jigsaw puzzle piece, fitting right in.

You seem to move most during a basketball game, she says. Thank you for your support!

And Mama swears you wriggle after a very spicy

meal, as if you can taste what she is tasting. *What to Expect* says you start tasting at twenty-seven weeks, and you are only about twenty weeks. But Mama says you probably have a sophisticated palate like the rest of the family.

WHAT I LOVE TO TASTE
Chili peppers
Sammy's enchilada casserole
Sammy's spaghetti with marinara sauce and meatballs
Mama's cakes
Sammy's pot roast
Sushi
Ice cream, not every flavor (e.g., not Blueberry Crumb)
Cotton candy (I've actually never tasted it, but I just know I'd like it.)
Cranberry relish
Mint picked fresh from our backyard
(Actually, the list of things to eat is very long.)
Rain on my tongue
Love,
Pen

PS. I wonder what acorn mush tastes like. I imagine it tastes like nuts.

SATURDAY, MARCH 21, 2015

Dear You,

Gabby and I walked over to Hazel's this afternoon. Her mom said Hazel was in her room, but when I started to go toward the big bedroom, I smelled cigarette smoke coming from under the door.

Her mom said, "No, no, not THAT room. The other one."

And then I knew why Hazel's eyes had been so red in school the other day. Her mom and Rick have moved themselves into the big master bedroom.

Hazel was sitting on her bed, which is now in the smaller room.

Hazel: "It all happened really fast after they had a big argument. The refrigerator is in the garage now. I told them its humming noise helps me sleep, but they said it doesn't really fit in this room. Rick says I've been spoiled."

Gabby: "You look like a spoiled grapefruit."

Me: "Or maybe a spoiled banana."

Hazel gave a little smile. "Ha ha, to both of you," she said.

Her voice was gravelly because her nose was stuffed up.

"My mom said I am allowed to listen to music on my iPad when I can't sleep. Also, my mom said I could paint this room any color I want. I am trying to make the best of things."

Hazel didn't really look like she was trying to make the best of things. Her books and Dubs posters and stuffed animals and shoes were scattered all over the room. There were plates of leftover food on the floor near her bed. She had been eating meals in her room. Her choice, she said.

Hazel hadn't even watched last night's game against the Pelicans. She hadn't felt like it. She must have been feeling really bad. She asked us how Klay Thompson was doing. We were sorry to have to tell her he was still out with his sore ankle, but we won the game because of Harrison Barnes, who scored twenty-two points.

So Hazel perked up. It is amazing how basketball can do that to you when you are down in the dumps!

Then Gabby had a great idea, as she usually does.

Gabby: "Hey, Penny and I can help you paint your room."

Me: "And guess what? We have paint samples at our house!"

I raced home and brought back the paint chips. Hazel chose Petunia Pink, which wouldn't have been my choice, but it's her room. Her mom said she would buy the paint. Gabby said there are brushes and a drop cloth in her garage. So we are all set to paint pretty soon.

We picked up everything from the floor and helped Hazel put her stuff away. We even sprayed with Febreze to get the cigarette smell out as much as we could.

Then we watched the game at Gabby's house. A win against the Jazz, 106–91.

We tried to mimic Andrew Bogut's Australian accent after we heard him interviewed. Gabby did it best. She is so talented! Lately, she is considering the acting profession.

Mike wasn't there. Gabby said he was over at a friend's house. I was very disappointed, of course. It would have been fun sharing the win with him.

Love,
Penny

SUNDAY, MARCH 22, 2015

Dear You,

And now for another installment of . . .

SECRETS OF THE SECRET STAIRWAY (SOSS)
LOVE AND MARRIAGE AND TRUTH EDITION

GABBY'S SECRET:

Gabby said she had gossip, not a secret. The news
is she is positive that Mike has a girlfriend. Lately, he
drives off by himself, probably to take the girlfriend on
dates. Gabby saw a Mounds candy wrapper in the car's
garbage receptacle, and Mike hates coconut.

Hazel and I laughed. We both feel that is not enough
evidence. It could have been anyone's Mounds bar! I
think Angel likes Mounds bars, actually.

So I am trying hard not to feel worried and jealous, because just because you are worried about
something doesn't mean it will happen.

HAZEL'S SECRET:

Hazel hopes her mother and Rick don't get married.

Rick is still not a goat lover, she said. Nell has never
nuzzled Rick's hair, not even once.

We told her that maybe Rick needs more time to get used to having a goat in his own backyard. Gabby said her dad didn't like their pet iguana at first, either.

Hazel began to cry. She said it's taking much too long. Her mother used to be a goat lover. She even made yogurt! Then she changed when she met Rick. Rick said that Nell may have to go. He wants to put a bocce court in the backyard. Bocce is sort of like outdoor bowling. A goat would be totally in the way of the bocce games.

I have so much more empathy for Hazel. Remember Mr. Chen's tie where one line looked smaller but really wasn't? It's sort of like that with Hazel. I saw her one way, but now I see her another way, even though she has been the same person all along.

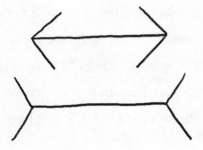

MY SECRET:
Right then and there, I decided it was OK to share my fabrication with Hazel.

I took a deep breath and admitted to her that I do not possess any Ohlone DNA, and that I had borrowed Sammy's heritage. Sammy is a relative by adoption and by domestic partnership only.

I told her the story about Mama and my deceased dad both being orphans and how that's why I didn't use my own heritage. I didn't really have any. And also I was envious of everyone else's interesting heritages in our class.

Hazel made me feel much better.

Hazel: "I can understand why you fabricated. I fabricate sometimes, too. Everyone does. I promise with all my heart not to tell. But how terribly tragic that your mom is an orphan! When I saw the movie about that orphan Annie, some parts of it made me sob, especially when she sang 'Tomorrow.'"

Gabby: "I thought it was so horrible that the orphans in the movie had to do all that mopping and scrubbing in the orphanage!"

I don't think Mama had to do a lot of mopping and scrubbing at her foster parents' homes. At least I hope not. I will have to remember to ask her.

I also gave Gabby and Hazel a preview of my presentation, the part about the Bay Street mall and the desecrated burial sites. We vowed never, ever to shop there again, even though the Apple Store is there.

After that, we just kept talking and talking some more. It felt so good to stretch my heart and mind. And have TWO really good friends to share private things with on our special Secret Stairway. Now I see how that works.

Love,

Penny

3/23/15: Beat the Wizards tonight, 107–76.

3/24/15: Beat the Portland Trail Blazers tonight, 122–108.

WEDNESDAY, MARCH 25, 2015

Dear You,

Today, Hazel said: "The Dubs are at the bottom of the NBA, you know."

Gabby and I: "What?"

Hazel: "It's true! In tattoo statistics! Curry and

Bogut have tattoos that are covered up or too small to notice. Klay Thompson and a few others don't have any at all."

We laughed our heads off about that.

You can find out anything on the Internet, anything at all.

Lucky duck Hazel has her very own iPad, as I told you. Her father bought it for her when her parents got a divorce, after he moved away. One day, she came home, and there it was, fresh from the online Apple Store!

Her mom's boyfriend, Rick, says it's outrageous that she has her own iPad. But Hazel says it's a gift from her own father and it's TOTALLY, TOTALLY none of Rick's business.

So Hazel goes on the Internet for her own research whenever she needs to. She doesn't need to go to the library or use a parent's computer like the rest of us. She kindly offered to share her iPad with Gabby and me.

Today, we were at Hazel's house after school, Hazel and Gabby and I, researching facts about our countries of origin: Russia, England, Jamaica, and the United States, specifically Oakland around the time of the early Ohlone.

And then Hazel said that she feels SO bad that Mama is an orphan. An orphan with no stories about her heritage! She thought we should search the Internet to get more information about Mama's family in Wyoming.

Mama didn't even own a computer back in Junoville, and that was a long time ago, I realized. Since then, she must have given up looking for relatives anywhere, out of sadness.

Hazel: "Even if they are dead relatives, which would make them ANCESTORS, it would still be interesting."

So I agreed, and all of a sudden we were researching real, live Wyoming people not only from Junoville, the tiny town where Mama is from, but all over the state. We felt like detectives!

We searched for people with Mama's maiden name, Doppel. I decided to check out Wolney, her married name with my father, too. Even if these people didn't have anything to do with Mama's relatives, maybe they'd know someone who did.

We found some Wolneys and Doppels, but they were dead ancestors. (There were quite a few obituaries online.) But we also found two living Doppels and four living Wolneys. A few were on the same baseball team and one shared a recipe and one was asking advice about her painful joints.

The hair on my arms stood up on end. It was exciting to see the names of potential relatives!

One big problem, though. There weren't any email addresses or even snail-mail addresses along with the names. But Hazel is a good detective, DOGGED and INTREPID (great detective words). And also more experienced on the Internet than I am. We just kept googling more pages, NEXT and NEXT, and soon we found:

An address for DOPPEL AND SMITH REAL ESTATE FIRM, and the website of THE DOPPEL COUNTRY COUSINS TRIO. There was a sample of their tunes to download and a P.O. address to order their CD.

And then we found an address in Junoville for FRESH FROM THE VINE, "jams lovingly stirred and safely preserved in Barbara Wolney's spotless kitchen." When you order three jars of jam, you get a FREE copy of a book of horse poems called *poems of hooves and the wind in my hair* by a locally famous poet.

Hazel: "Ouch. Are the hooves in his hair? A comma is definitely needed after the word hooves."

Gabby: "No capital letters in the title! Mr. Chen would correct that with his red pen."

Anyway, we are going to write some letters tomorrow, even though I'm not going to order a CD or jam.

Love,

Penny

THURSDAY, MARCH 26, 2015

Dear You,

I mailed my letters, three of them. Gabby and Hazel helped me with the wording. Then I copied our rough draft onto my golden retriever stationery three times. I spent a lot of time and effort on them. I tried to make my handwriting neat and legible, and I think I succeeded. I checked all the spelling.

All three letters were the same except for the salutations:

DEAR_____ (INSERT EITHER DOPPEL AND SMITH REAL ESTATE FIRM, THE DOPPEL COUNTRY COUSINS TRIO, or FRESH FROM THE VINE),

I AM PENELOPE VICTORIA BACH. I AM IN FIFTH GRADE.

I REQUIRE INFORMATION ABOUT MY DISTANT RELATIVES.

MY MOTHER IS REBECCA BACH, FORMERLY DOPPEL AND THEN WOLNEY, FROM JUNOVILLE. MY FATHER WAS WILLIAM WOLNEY, DECEASED IN A MOTORCYCLE ACCIDENT IN OAKLAND, FORMERLY OF JUNOVILLE, TOO. BOTH OF THEM WERE ORPHANS.

THEY MOVED TO OAKLAND, CALIFORNIA, IN 2002.

THANKS IN ADVANCE FOR YOUR HELP!

BY THE WAY, I AM AN AVID BASKETBALL FAN. I HAVE NOTICED THAT WYOMING DOESN'T HAVE A PROFESSIONAL BASKETBALL TEAM. MY CONDO-LENCES ABOUT THAT.

EMPATHICALLY YOURS,

PVB

Hazel and Gabby agreed it would be a shock for Mama to get the news herself in the mail, out of the blue, so Hazel said we should give her address as a return address instead of mine. Hazel always gets the mail before her mom or Rick come home. Then Hazel will give me the mail from any long-lost rela-tives, and I can break the good news to Mama with sensitivity.

Love,

Pen

3/27/15: A rout against the
Grizzlies, 107–84.

TUESDAY, MARCH 31, 2015

Dear You,

Today, there is no school, because it is Cesar Chavez Day.

Our class has been learning about Cesar Chavez. He was born on this day in 1927 and died in 1993.

He defended farm workers' right not to have to work around pesticides and their right to make more money. He helped them join together and form unions so they could be stronger together.

Chavez used to say "Sí, se puede," which means "Yes, it can be done." Mr. Chen pointed out that President Obama used "Yes, we can!" for his election campaign slogan. I thought President Obama had made that up.

Maybe he did, but it just goes to show that there is nothing new under the sun, like Mama always says.

Cesar Chavez used to go on hunger strikes to prove his points and get attention for his ethical, righteous causes. ETHICAL means things that are right rather than wrong.

I can't stop thinking about those hunger strikes! That is something I don't think I could ever do. Neither does Gabby. But Hazel says of course we could, if something was important enough.

We beat the Clippers, 110–106 (even though Draymond Green wasn't there because his shin is inflamed).

What a winning streak! We know we've made the playoffs, but it still feels good to win.

Feel better, Draymond!

Happy Festus Ezeli Day!

By the way, you are as big as a small seedless watermelon. Mama's belly is round with you.

Love,

Pen

WEDNESDAY, APRIL 1, 2015

Dear You,

On the basketball list this morning: HERMIONE GRANGER. (APRIL FOOL!)

Ha! As if Kenny's other names were real.

I finally decided to tell him we suspected it was him.

Kenny: "Moi?"

Then he said something surprising: "Hey, I apologize for making fun of your name. Can we call a truce?"

But I said I wasn't angry with him. So how could we call a truce?

Kenny: "Really? You're not angry with me? That's good."

Disdain for his immaturity is not the same as anger. I should have said that, but I didn't think of it at the time.

Gabby, Hazel, and I keep trying to copy Steph Curry's behind-the-back dribble in the schoolyard. It's harder than it looks. In other words, we can't do it.

But we killed at HORSE after school! We decided to join in because, even though we can't do that move, we are better than ever from practicing our shots. The boys grumbled that we weren't any good, but Kenny Walinhoff said, "Oh, let them play! They'll be out pretty fast."

He didn't know how good we are. And then we showed 'em! Gabby won once and Hazel and I each almost won.

Kenny, CONDESCENDINGLY (that means he felt superior to us): "You girls have been practicing! Keep it up!"

Gabby, Hazel, and I all looked at him disdainfully.

Love,

Penny

THURSDAY, APRIL 2, 2015

Dear You,

A nail-biter against the Suns tonight, but we won! 107–106!

WHAT I LOVE TO HEAR

Oakland fans ROARING—

THE WARRIORS HAVE WON THE LAST ELEVEN GAMES IN A ROW!!!

WHAT ELSE I LOVE TO HEAR

Our family singing

"Choices (Yup)" by E-40 (Warriors remix)

"Live Like a Warrior" by Matisyahu

Rain on the roof

Video game sound effects

Popcorn popping

Mike's voice, which is almost like music

Wind chimes

Fountains running on a hot day

Uncle Ziggy's motorcycle pulling up

Do you hear us out here, You?

Did you hear me cheering? Especially when Harrison Barnes got that shot with only 0.4 seconds left in the game?

Did you hear the police sirens roaring down Park Boulevard?

Did you hear Sammy drop that empty cast-iron pot on her toe and yell "fiddlesticks"?

I wonder.

But Mama says you can definitely hear her insides swishing like ocean waves and her heart beating, all the time. Like a lullaby with a drumbeat, Mama says.

Lucky you.

Love,

Me

FRIDAY, APRIL 3, 2015

Dear You,

The whole class was giggly and silly today, even Mr. Chen.

Here is his tie:

That's because today was the last day before spring break!

CORRECTION:

Hazel wasn't giggly and silly. She came to school with her eyes swollen and red again.

I asked her to please tell me what was wrong, but she declined. She put on that big smile of hers and said everything was OK.

But I saw her smile disappear when she thought I wasn't looking.

At the end of the day, Mr. Chen said that the time off would be a good opportunity to find recipes representing our heritages. And, if we can, we should bring the cooked dish during the last week of class in June for our GRADUATION . . .

Mr. Chen: "PARTY!"

He did some dance moves that were pretty cool.

Everyone in the class cheered and did copycat dance moves. Some cool, some not.

I will get a recipe from Grandma Lorraine and Great-Grandma Grace.

I have been reading more about what the early Ohlone ate. I am no longer worried that they didn't have enough to eat. Nobody went hungry! There was SO much to eat! Not only that, but there was NO junk food to block their arteries, hee-hee.

The men hunted bear and deer and other animals. They caught ducks and geese and gathered their eggs. They fished for salmon and trout and smelt and scooped up many kinds of shellfish—mussels, clams, oysters, crabs, abalone, and more. YUM!

The women gathered the plant foods—acorns, seeds, nuts, mushrooms, grasses, clover, and sea-weed. They knew how to recognize and separate out the poisonous parts. And there were so many acorns, the Ohlone didn't even have to farm! I already mentioned the delicious acorn mush.

Now I'm hungry.

Love,

Penny

PS. Hazel told me what was wrong. Rick will be

making her do more chores over the break. She says he is not quite as bad as Miss Hannigan, the head of the orphanage in Little Orphan Annie's story, but it's close. I feel so bad for Hazel.

SATURDAY, APRIL 4, 2015

Dear You,
Sadly, You, I have to tell you that life has its ups and its downs.

It was a disheartening day.

Disappointing news about Mama's heritage. Hazel gave me a flyer from the Doppel and Smith Real Estate Firm that she had hidden in her sock drawer. It came in the mail yesterday, all the way from Cheyenne, Wyoming. Doppel and Smith must have sent it as soon as they received my letter.

It was not a personal response in ANY way:

Example: "32 YEARS OF REAL ESTATE EXCELLENCE!"

Believe me, I checked it over very carefully, upside down and inside out. And there was no card or letter along with it—I waved the envelope around a few times just in case.

We went over to Gabby's for dinner and to watch

the game. The Mavericks couldn't break our winning streak. We won 123–110.

I casually asked where Mike was.

Gabby said she is absolutely positive he went to watch the game with his new girlfriend. She gave us some more clues:

He put on his new jeans, which he wouldn't wear just for his guy friends.

She thinks he has a new aftershave. It smells like peppermint and roses.

He won't say exactly where he is going. Just "out."

He mentioned he definitely won't have time to coach us, because he is too busy, especially on the weekends.

She swears she wasn't snooping but she saw I HEART L written on a piece of paper on his desk.

Those sounded like very good clues to Hazel and me.

And that is why it has been an especially disHEART-ening day.

My heart feels bruised. I think my heart will hurt because of Mike for a very long time.

Maybe forever.

Love,

Pen

SUNDAY, APRIL 5, 2015

Dear You,

I hate the drought. But today, we had a few show-ers, with more expected, VERY unusual for April.

I suggested to Sammy that maybe the Dubs are bringing us the rain, because of their twelve-game winning streak. Sammy called that "superstitious magical thinking." She said that basketball wins have nothing to do with unusual weather patterns, which are very complicated and scientifically based. Of course, I said. I was only kidding (sort of).

BUT then the luck of the Dubs changed. They LOST to the Spurs, 92–107. So there goes my superstitious climate theory. After a twelve-game winning streak, Dubs blew a DOUBLE-DIGIT halftime lead!

And then Sammy said she couldn't understand why I'm so upset. It's just a one-game slump, and after all, we already know the Dubs are in the play-offs. She asked if there was something else besides basketball bugging me.

I decided to share with Mama and Sammy that I like Mike, but he has a girlfriend his own age, which, of course, makes sense. I told them my heart hurt terribly.

Mama: "Oh, hon. Believe me, a wonderful aspect of life is that time heals. You'll see."

I think Dr. Time has a big job on its hands. Now I understand why there are so many heartbreaking songs about love. Except I really don't feel like singing.

Pen

MONDAY, APRIL 6, 2015

Dear You,

SECRETS OF THE SECRET STAIRWAY (SOSS)
EMERGENCY EDITION

GABBY'S SECRET:
Gabby said she didn't have any secrets at that point in time.

MY SECRET:
I said that I no longer had a secret love because of certain sad circumstances, which shall remain private. I saw Gabby looking at me in a funny way. I wondered if she was reading my mind.

HAZEL'S SECRET:

My secret was sad, but what Hazel told us was TRAGIC.

Her mom said Nell the goat has to be given away as soon as possible!!! Rick wants to start putting in the bocce court so he can have people over for backyard cocktails. A goat would probably try to eat the hors d'oeuvres.

So Nell will be donated to someone else, or farmed out to one of those companies that hires goats to eat grass on hillsides near the noisy freeways. Those poor sweet goats always look so bored and lonely, just chomping away all day.

But who will hug Nell after her hard day on the hillsides? Who will whisper things to her and listen to her wheezy secrets and sounds of comfort? How will we find out how Nell is doing?

And Nell is a member of a family! We tried to imagine a family giving away one of their children. It was IMPOSSIBLE to imagine.

It's mostly because Rick isn't a goat lover, we decided. Actually, the situation is worse than that. He is a GOATIST.

That's not a real word. Still. It fits.

Hazel said she phoned her father in Cincinnati and asked if she and Nell could go live with him. He refused. She is heartbroken.

Gabby and I are heartbroken, too.

Sending away Nell, a family member, is unethical, we all decided.

It felt like an emergency. And so we immediately began our hunger strike, inspired by the late Cesar Chavez.

All three of us. Because that's what friends are for. We vowed not to eat until Rick and Hazel's mom promise to keep Nell.

Hazel was right, Gabby and I agreed. It is easy to decide to go on a hunger strike when something is very important to you.

That was at eleven in the morning.

I didn't eat lunch.

Later, I didn't even have an afternoon snack, even though Mama had baked an upside-down apple cake, and there it was sitting on the kitchen counter, smelling so good.

But . . .

of ALL days, Sammy made her famous spaghetti with marinara sauce and garlic-parmesan meatballs for dinner. Wait until you taste those meatballs, You! They are IRRESISTIBLE.

IRRESISTIBLE means I couldn't help eating some. I took a very tiny portion of pasta and sauce and only one meatball.

Sammy: "What's the matter? One measly meatball? Aren't you hungry?"

Mama: "She must be sick!"

And I said, yes, I wasn't feeling so good, but it was because of Nell. I told them the whole story and that I was hunger striking.

Sammy and Mama said that a hunger strike wouldn't help things anyway and that kids have absolutely no business going on hunger strikes.

And after that, I ate some more spaghetti and four more garlic-parmesan meatballs. I just couldn't help it, even though Gabby and Hazel were hunger striking and I was letting them down by failing at it.

NOT a great day.

Love,

Pen

PS. But I did skip Sundae Monday tonight. Chocolate Banana. I'm sure it was delicious.

PPS. I have even more respect for Cesar Chavez at this point in time.

TUESDAY, APRIL 7, 2015

Dear You,

Gabby and Hazel found food irresistible yesterday, too.

Gabby's dad was grilling steak, and the barbecue smell did her in. Hazel couldn't help eating her mother's turkey meatloaf, and it isn't even her favorite food. Liza puts hardboiled eggs down the middle of it, and they get sort of beige-colored after baking, Hazel says. You have to eat extremely carefully around the beige hardboiled eggs if you don't happen to like them mixed in with meatloaf, which Hazel doesn't. But she was so hungry, she even ate one of those eggs!

Hunger is so powerful.

Do you ever feel hungry, You? Maybe you don't, since you are fed continuously inside Mama.

Gabby suggested that when the time comes, we should have a Totally Goatally goodbye party for Nell. Party hats for everyone, even Nell, and streamers and chocolate cupcakes (for us) and alfalfa cupcakes (for Nell) and a garland of flowers around Nell's neck. Which she'd eat, of course, but so what? It's her party.

HAZEL: "The time will NOT come. I will make sure of it!"

She didn't tell us how she would do that, but her eyes were slits and her mouth was a straight line, and she looked like she meant it. That made me feel hopeful for Nell.

Love,

Pen

THURSDAY, APRIL 9, 2015

Dear You,

Gabby and Hazel and I are so inspired. We keep practicing Curry's behind-the-back fancy impossible dribble. Just because it's fun. (But we still can't do it.)

We have begun painting Hazel's bedroom Petunia

Pink. It is going quickly. There is still a faint smell of cigarette smoke.

Speaking of color, I read that your hair is white, like a little old man's (or woman's!). PIGMENT is a substance in the hair that gives it its color, and you don't have any of that yet.

My hair is brown—the color of cocoa before you add water for hot chocolate. So is Mama's. We have to wait and see about yours.

PIGMENT has nothing at all to do with pigs. Words are so weird.

Love,

Pen

A win tonight against the Blazers, 116–105!

Curry beat his three-point record from two years ago. A shoo-in for MOST VALUABLE PLAYER (MVP)!!!!!

Dear You,

Grandma Lorraine and Great-Grandma Grace love learning new words, just like I do. They told me that the language of the Chochenyo Ohlone is also called Chochenyo, and the modern-day Ohlone are relearning it in classes and from old recordings. It is so sad to think of a language dying. But it makes me feel hopeful to know that a language can be brought back to life by people wanting to remember it with all their hearts and souls.

They told me that "mele" means both grandmother and great-grandmother. They said I could call them that if I like, so I will.

Mele Grace: "Timli!" And she put some salmon on my plate.

Once I knew the salmon's Chochenyo name, TIMLI, it tasted very special. Can a word really make a difference?

But it could also be because Mele Grace only buys salmon born in the river, and she smokes manzanita branches on her barbecue for flavor, in the old way. There is a small manzanita bush on the hill behind their house. Mele Grace also pours hot water over the manzanita berries to make tea and makes a manzanita berry juice for salad dressing.

I asked Mele Grace and Mele Lorraine if they made acorn flour from acorns gathered from the California oak tree on their front lawn. They giggled at that question.

Mele Lorraine: "Who has the time?"

As I said, the early Ohlone women spent days and days making their flour. I just thought I'd ask anyway.

Mele Lorraine and Mele Grace didn't gather the lettuces and mushrooms for our salad from the wild either. They buy those at Berkeley Bowl. But Mele Grace made the manzanita salad dressing. And we sipped delicious hot manzanita tea while we watched the game tonight.

We beat Minnesota 110–101. Mele Lorraine and Mele Grace thought it was terrific that we won, but I told them the Dubs are usually much sharper.

When Mama and Sammy came to pick me up, Mele Lorraine said she would make acorn flour from scratch with me. She has friends who do that in the autumn, when the acorns are in season in the woods. I am looking forward to that.

Mama and Sammy can't believe my "incredible enthusiasm" for learning the Ohlone ways. I am surprised to write this, but I am quite enthusiastic about giving my presentation. It's going to be a good one, and I have important things to say.

Love,

Me

SUNDAY, APRIL 12, 2015

Dear You,

Happy Andrew Bogut Day once again.

We are almost finished painting Hazel's room. No more cigarette smell, unless you stand very still and sniff like an experienced Ohlone from long ago. Or maybe what I'm smelling is just a bad memory.

Petunia Pink looks prettier than it sounds.

Love,

Pen

MONDAY, APRIL 13, 2015

Dear You,

Back to school today. Same old stuff.

Except that something happened that is worrying me a bit.

More than a bit.

I am upset, actually.

Mr. Chen had that look on his face that all teachers have after breaks from their classrooms. Rested and happy. Sometimes, it's hard to tell whether the teachers are happy to see us or if they are just thinking happy thoughts about their fun vacations. Probably both. And they usually have new clothes and shoes from all that extra time they have had to shop. Here is Mr. Chen's new tie:

But here is what is upsetting me:

Rested and happy, Mr. Chen said he'd had a brain-storm over the break.

Mr. Chen: "I am looking forward to hearing your presentations about your heritages in June. But my colleagues and I think the younger students will also benefit from them. They will have similar heritage projects as they advance through the upper grades."

Mr. Chen: "I will invite other interested class-rooms, as well as Mrs. Solomon and her office staff!"

Mrs. Solomon is the SCHOOL PRINCIPAL, You!

But there was more.

Mr. Chen: "And, of course, you can invite any of your parents who are able to attend. Then, after the presentations, we will have that rip-roaring party I promised you, with your heritage dishes and some carefully chosen junk food. Grand Presentation Day will be on June 10."

"YAY!" shouted the whole class, except me.

Tonight, the Dubs beat the Grizzlies, 111–107. Klay Thompson scored an amazing forty-two points. I didn't think about my worries during the game, but then I remembered as soon as the game was over.

What if other parents mention their own invitations to Mama and Sammy? What do I tell them? I don't want them there to hear my false presentation!

But I DO want them there. I am heartbroken at the thought of giving my presentation without them in the audience. I would feel like an orphan.

I don't know what to do. I am in a terrible quandary. QUANDARY is another word I have always wanted to use, but certainly not for a personal reason.

Love,

Penny

TUESDAY, APRIL 14, 2015

Dear You,

Presenting today's installment of:

SECRETS OF THE SECRET STAIRWAY (SOSS)
THE SAD, SCARED, AND SIBLING EDITION

HAZEL'S SECRET:

Rick has put an ad in Craigslist for Nell's adoption.

Hazel is trying very hard to sabotage his plans. She answered Rick's cell a few times and informed the callers that Nell had already been given away.

Also, she quietly tells interested people who come to meet the goat that Nell has a terrible bowel problem, as well as chronic indigestion. Nell's burps smell like rotten eggs, she says.

Nell is such a beautiful, healthy animal! If Nell was a human being, Hazel's lies about her would be SLANDEROUS. But we all agree that the slanderous lies are for a protective, ethical reason.

GABBY'S SECRET:

Gabby said that sometimes she gets so angry

with Angel, she wishes she didn't have a little sister. Sometimes, not always.

"I feel sorry for you," I said, "having a little sister who is a pest and no angel." I told her I hope I don't feel that way about my new sibling, and I probably won't.

Gabby laughed when I said this.

Gabby: "How do you know your new sibling won't be a pest? Most younger siblings are."

"I just know," I said.

"We'll see," said Gabby. And we sort of agreed to disagree.

MY SECRET:

It helped to talk about my quandary. Hazel and Gabby had some advice.

Gabby: "If your parents find out about the Grand Presentation Day, you can always stay home with the flu, and they'd never find out what you were going to talk about."

Hazel: "But even if they aren't there, I think you have some important information to share with your audience. The presentation must go on."

I did feel better. And I don't really have to worry about it for a while.

COUNTDOWN TO AUDITORIUM PRESENTATION:
Fifty-eight days.

Love,

Penny

WEDNESDAY, APRIL 15, 2015

Dear You,

We keep checking our basketball list on the bulletin board. Some days, we don't check because we figure nothing has changed. And nothing has. Our names are still on them, and also that girl Candy, and the crossed-out fake names. Not even any new fake names, lately.

ADMISSION: I even miss finding fake names.

It is a sad fact, but nobody looks at old announcements and ads after a while. I see them on bulletin boards at the supermarket all the time, torn and faded. All those lost dogs or cats or birds! Are they ever found?

Love,

Penelope

THURSDAY, APRIL 16, 2015

Dear You,

We beat Hazel's old team, the Nuggets, last night, 133–126. Klay Thompson scored twenty-five points!

Hazel felt she had to remind us again that she's a Dubs fan now, through and through. Don't worry, we told her, we know, we know.

We are so grateful that we have basketball to take our minds off our worries about goats, fabrications, pesty sisters, and bruised hearts. The games really help with life's bittersweetness.

So did you hear me shrieking, You? Dubs fans are big shriekers.

Uncle Ziggy said that coaches from other teams have complained that the "decibel level" in Oracle Arena probably isn't legal.

Sour grapes, I say!

The regular season is over.

NOW LET THE PLAYOFFS BEGIN!

We are marching to victory, You!

TUESDAY, APRIL 21, 2015

Dear You,
Something bad happened, but I don't feel like writing about it now.
Love,
Penny

WEDNESDAY, APRIL 22, 2015

Dear You,
Don't feel like writing today.
Love,
Pen

FRIDAY, APRIL 24, 2015

Dear You,
I am still here. I will write tomorrow.
xxx, Penny

SATURDAY, APRIL 25, 2015

Dear You,
Something bad has happened.

It has been a while since I've written, You.

Each time I picked up my pencil, I chewed on it for a long time. Then I ended up not writing anything at all.

Because something bad has happened.

It is not about basketball or my project in case you are wondering. It is not about Mike maybe having a girlfriend, even though that's not a *maybe* anymore.

Of course, you are not wondering, but tonight the Dubs beat the Pelicans on the Pelicans' home court, for their fourth straight win, to win the series. But even the games can't help me take my mind off this.

Because what happened last week is mostly what I'm thinking about. I can't stop thinking about it.

Mama and Sammy keep saying I should write about it. They said maybe writing will help.

Maybe tomorrow.

Showers today. The day felt teary, like me.

Love,

Pen

SUNDAY, APRIL 26, 2015

Dear You,

My memory of what happened is a giant black blur with big red flashes, but I will try.

It happened last Sunday, a whole week ago. It feels like yesterday.

Mike picked up Gabby and me from Hazel's house in his father's car. We had been putting the finishing touches on Hazel's Petunia Pink bedroom. We needed Mike's help because we had brushes and a drop cloth to carry back home and also it was getting dark.

Mike put everything in his trunk, even the empty paint cans, which he kindly said he would recycle for us.

A girl was sitting in the front passenger seat. Yes, Gabby was right. Mike has a girlfriend. Her name is Lee-Anne. She has long hair like ocean waves and she wears jangly gold bracelets and her perfume smells like peppermint and roses. She has very long legs and plays basketball in high school.

She calls Mike "Michael."

Michael looked so happy.

Gabby and I were quiet, because it was a new thing to be with Mike and a girlfriend. I was pondering the fact that a person is supposed to be happy when that person's loved one is happy. But I wasn't happy that Mike was happy, and did that mean I didn't feel true love?

Of course, I'm digressing. I guess I don't want to write about what came next.

My memory is not as big a blur as I thought.

I actually remember everything, now that I'm writing it down.

The sky was gray and pink. We had just turned off Park Boulevard, and Lee-Anne asked us all if we wanted some gum. Mike took a piece. Gabby and I both said no, thank you very much.

And Mike looked into his rearview mirror then and grinned at us, because we were so quiet and shy. I was still pondering whether my love was true, etcetera.

Then, all of a sudden, Mike's happy eyes changed direction, and he was looking back, but not at us. And he said, very softly, "Uh-oh."

The flashing red lights of the police car filled up our own car, even though the police car was in back of us. The siren went WHOOP!

Mike signaled and pulled over and stopped.

Lee-Anne: "Hands on the wheel, Michael. Remember, stay cool."

The cop tapped on the window. Mike rolled it down. Then Mike put his hands back on the steering wheel.

Cop to Mike: "You were going pretty fast, kid. Get out of the car!"

Me: "Why?"

Gabby: "Shut up, Penny!"

She was whispering. She poked me in the ribs with her elbow, hard.

Mike got out of the car. He gave the cop his driver's license. The cop made Mike face the car and put his hands on the roof. He patted him down. That is called FRISKING. Like a criminal.

He told Mike to spit out his gum. Right there on the street, like a litterer.

Mike is a good guy! I wanted to tell that cop. Mike catches spiders in his house very gently in tissues and shakes them free! That's how good a guy he is!

Cop: "What are you kids doing speeding around this neighborhood at night?"

Mike: "Just going home, officer."

Me: "We weren't speeding!"

This time it was Lee-Anne: "Please be quiet, Penny."

Then the cop told Mike to open the trunk, and he did.

Cop: "You kids doing graffiti with this paint?"

Mike: "No, sir. It's for painting a bedroom."

We could hear the cop thumping the paint cans around in the trunk and looking under the drop cloth.

Maybe he realized that Petunia Pink isn't a good graffiti color, because he slammed the trunk door shut and went back to his cop car.

His radio crackled and spluttered and had a conversation with itself, and then he was back. He wrote out a speeding ticket and gave it to Mike.

Mike wasn't speeding, You! I was a witness. But I didn't say that out loud.

"Am I free to go, officer?" Mike asked.

Cop: "Yes. Watch your speed."

Nobody spoke on the way home. They dropped me off.

The next day, Gabby told Hazel and me that Mike had been so proud of getting his driver's license, but now he has a ticket for speeding, and that is called a moving violation, even though Mike didn't violate a single thing. He will have to go to driver's ed. And his dad's car insurance will go up!

Gabby said Mike cried. He didn't cry in front of Lee-Anne, of course. Only at home with his family.

And then Gabby said that when you are black, you don't only learn how to signal and stop and parallel park. You learn to keep your hands on the wheel when you are stopped by a cop, especially a white cop. To be really calm. No twitchiness! To be as polite as can be.

Sometimes, you may have to say, "Officer, I know my rights."

Or even, "Officer, please don't shoot."

I told Gabby not to exaggerate. I don't know why I said that, because I do remember all those incidents on the news. I really do!

But I said it. It just popped out.

"Don't exaggerate, Gabby." I will never, ever forget that I said such a dumb thing.

Maybe I didn't want her to talk about bad things like that.

About RACISTS. Racists are people who don't like other people because of the color of their skin.

Maybe I didn't even want to believe it myself.

Gabby told me to grow up, and she started to cry right there in the schoolyard.

I wish I hadn't said what I said to Gabby.

Things have felt shivery cold between me and her all week. I did say I was sorry once, but she didn't answer. She is not talking to Hazel, either. I guess because Hazel just stood there and didn't say a single word to her.

I should have said something else. I'm not sure what, but NOT that Gabby was exaggerating. Gabby never exaggerates. She always speaks the honest truth.

I am so sad, even though the Warriors had a playoff sweep against the Pelicans.

Love,

Penny

SAME DAY, AFTERNOON

Dear You,

There was a gigantic earthquake in Nepal. Mama and Sammy were crying when they heard about it on the news. Many people have died.

I phoned Gabby to talk to her, but her mom said she was busy.

I phoned Hazel. She said to come over. We will talk about what to do and maybe Nell can help.

How can Nell help? I wondered.

There was a terrible earthquake in Nepal, so I am ashamed to write this next sentence.

So I will write it very small.

IT WILL FEEL LIKE AN EARTHQUAKE IF I LOSE MY GOOD FRIEND!!!!!!

I told Mama and Sammy how ashamed I am to compare my friendship problems to a terrible earthquake.

Yes, Sammy said, it is all relative. But it is human and OK to feel sad about both things at once.

Love,

Pen

SAME DAY, NIGHT

Dear You,

What to Expect says you are beginning to take small practice breaths from your nose. I don't think you can smell yet, but who is to say?

You will love Nell and love the way she smells, like I do. She does NOT smell like rotten eggs!

And, also, you will enjoy hugging her. (Once, I saw a T-shirt that said HUG A TREE. I want one that says HUG A GOAT.) And brushing her and feeding her and milking her. Then hugging her again and smelling that goaty smell—earth and straw and, OK, poop, but in a good way.

Hazel had invited Gabby and me over, but I was the only one who came.

Me, hugging Nell: "Nell just made a suggestion to me."

Hazel: "I knew she'd do that! She gives me suggestions, too. What did she say?"

Me: "She said 'M-ah-ah-ah! Try, try, again.' I think she is suggesting we try to get Gabby to forgive us. Well, me, anyway, even though she's lumping us both together."

So Hazel and I wrote a letter on Hazel's stationery (hers has basketballs in the margins). We apologized profusely. We asked her to forgive us. We said that we didn't understand before, but now we do. We reminded her that we are the Three Splash Sisters, and Steph Curry and Klay Thompson probably have fights, too.

We went over to Gabby's house. Lee-Anne answered the door. I guess she is over there a lot. Then Mike came to the door, too. He smiled kindly at us. He yelled "Penny and Hazel are here!" to Gabby in another room.

But Gabby yelled back, "TELL THEM I'M BUSY!"

Lee-Anne: "Give her time, guys, OK?"

Me: "Tell her we are waiting for her today. She knows where to find us. At the SS. Tell her that. The SS. And please give her this letter."

Lee-Anne: "I will talk to her. Keep your chins up."

So Hazel and I waited at the Secret Stairway.

Hazel: "How much time should we give her?"

Me: "A lot."

Time heals all, Mama says. Time and paint made the cigarette smell go away in Hazel's bedroom (mostly). My heartache about Mike is a little bit less. But how long does it take to get a really good friend to believe you when you say you are sorry that you said something dumb?

We waited.

And waited.

I am not sure how long we waited, but it sure felt like a long time. It seemed like the sun had crawled closer to the west since we'd sat down on those stairs. We were getting worried.

But then we heard the trash cans clunking!

And there was Gabby coming up the stairs!

We all hugged and did victory fist bumps, and Hazel and I apologized for saying something stupid.

Gabby said thank you for understanding. Hazel said that's what friends are for.

We sat on the stairs and we talked about the Warriors' first-round sweep against the New Orleans Pelicans, which we hadn't done yet, and it felt so good. How Jrue Holiday of the Pelicans and Justin Holiday of the Warriors are brothers. That must be so hard! And all those three-pointers and assists and rebounds! Our defense! Green and Bogut going after Anthony Davis, that scary good Pelican! Four wins in the books, twelve to go, and maybe they'll be the NBA CHAMPS!

Then Gabby told us she had decided to be a policewoman when she is old enough. A fair and honest one.

She wondered if Steph Curry or Klay Thompson or Draymond Green had ever gotten stopped by the Oakland cops for speeding.

Hazel: "Only if they WERE speeding."

Me: "You don't get stopped when you're super famous."

Gabby: "But maybe BEFORE they were super famous."

It felt so different to think about the Dubs before they were super famous.

Yes, they were probably stopped, we all agreed.

Then we all went over to hug Nell and felt even better. It is amazing how good it feels to hug a goat.

I guess I have been trying to make you think that life is more sweet than bitter, You. Not the other way around. Sometimes, it's the other way around, and there's not a whole lot we can do about it. Sometimes. I promise to always tell you the truth, You.

So it was not a good week. BUT we swept the series! And Gabby is a Splash Sister again! That's pretty sweet.

Love,

Penny

TUESDAY, APRIL 28, 2015

Dear You,

Today is a very important, AWESOME, special day.

"History is being made," Mama said.

Sammy: "A wonderful lawyer, Mary Bonauto, is

173

arguing before the Supreme Court for same-sex marriage across the land. We won't know the verdict for a while, but we are so hopeful."

Then Mama and Sammy looked at each other as if they were reading each other's mind. I figured I knew what they were thinking.

Me: "Hooray! You're thinking of getting married!"

And right away, I made an excellent suggestion: "How about a wedding and then a big celebration after, with radish roses and tiny quiche hors d'oeuvres catered by Gabby's aunty Lue?"

They both smiled.

Sammy: "We will have a celebration when the baby is born."

Me: "Like a wedding, right?"

"Like a party," Mama said. "We will have lots to celebrate."

I hadn't read their minds after all.

Mama: "Don't worry, sweetie. I can tell that you are worried because we are not married. But Sammy and I have made sure all our rights are protected legally in California. We are both the full-fledged parents of our kids, we have family visitation rights in case one of us is in the hospital, our property is ours as a couple, and we are in each other's wills.

But gay couples in other states aren't as protected as we are. So it is a good thing to have the federal protection that the Supreme Court decision will give. And Sammy and I are very happy with a marriage of—"

Me: "I know. The heart."

Still.

Love,

P

WEDNESDAY, APRIL 29, 2015

Dear You,

It is your twenty-sixth week, and *What to Expect* says your eyes are beginning to open. I really didn't know that they were fused shut for the past few months.

FUSED! What a word!

Poor you with eyes fused shut!!!!!!!

But I guess there is not much to see in the darkness, is there?

Shadows?

Light from the outside getting in?

I will never know, and you will never tell me.

I can only imagine it. I would hate it if my eyes were fused.

WHAT I LOVE TO SEE

NATURE (which includes everything outdoors, for instance, the sky, sunrises and sunsets, the ocean, trees, flowers, parks, etcetera. Sorry—there is just too much good stuff to name, and you will understand when you get here. I try to honor all I see in nature, just like the Ohlone did and still do.)

Smiles

Raindrops on the window (oops, see NATURE)

Curry's three-pointers, Green's great defense, Bogut getting the rebounds

Nell, any part of her

Mike, my heart still flutters

A bowl of spaghetti with marinara sauce and garlic-parmesan meatballs when I'm hungry

Mr. Chen's ties

That's it for now, but, of course, there is much more to see in our big, big world.

Love,

Penny

THURSDAY, APRIL 30, 2015

Dear You,

The month of May, coming up, is my birthday month. I was born on May 16, 2004. You will be born sometime in July or August 2015.

Mama's birthday is in May, too, the day before mine. We always celebrate together. Usually, we even share a cake. I guess you can say that our birthdays are sort of merged.

But Mama said that she will not intrude on my birthday this year. I will be the big ONE-ONE, and I'm way past due for my own party and my own cake. I told her I never felt she was intruding (or vice versa) because it always felt cool and cozy to share a BD (birthday) with Mama. But I admit I feel a bit differently, now that I'm almost eleven.

Maybe Hazel will get some information about Mama's relatives or ancestors in Wyoming. That would be a nice birthday gift for Mama.

Everything depends on jam maker Barbara Wolney and the Doppel Country Cousins Trio now.

We are planning a party and sleepover for my own birthday. It will be great.

I also requested (1) a magician and (2) maybe a few fireworks in the backyard. Mama and Sammy nixed both ideas: (1) babyish (I think I agree) (2) dangerous and probably illegal.

Then I suggested bowling and arcade games at Plank at Jack London Square before the sleepover. I do love their Nacho Stack. They show basketball games on humongous screens while you bowl and they bring your food right to your bowling lane.

Again, nixed by the Parents. Too expensive. "What about a cheaper bowling alley?" they asked. But I don't really like bowling that much, so I declined.

Sammy suggested a trip to the Oakland Museum of California to see the replica of the Ohlone basket.

Me, flabbergasted: "FOR MY BIRTHDAY???"

I told her that's a good idea for research, but not a birthday trip. It would be mixing business with pleasure.

COUNTDOWN TO PRESENTATION: Forty-two days. Mama and Sammy are still in the dark about it.

Happy Steph Curry Day.

Love,

Penny

SATURDAY, MAY 2, 2015

Dear You,

I told Mr. Chen I planned to go to the Oakland Museum of California to do some further research—and also to celebrate my birthday. I just blurted that out. I knew it would impress him. He raised his eyebrows and wriggled them. His eyes beamed sparkles at me.

I told Mama and Sammy to take me and my friends to the museum for my birthday trip. They did that eyebrow-raising wriggling thing, too.

I guess I'm glad that's settled.

I am working very hard on my presentation. I will make it the very best it can be. I am sad that Mama and Sammy won't be there to hear it. They would be proud of me. (But not proud that I fabricated, of course.)

I have written quite a bit of information in my poodle notebook. I also traced some drawings from a book. It is much, much easier to trace and copy something than to draw it from scratch.

For example, here is an Ohlone tule house.

TULE means a kind of grass or bulrush that grew

in the marshy wetlands of that time long ago. There was much more water then, just as Mr. Chen pointed out.

Bundles of dried tule were tied around willow poles bent into a circle shape. These houses were warm and waterproof. They were easy to build quickly and weren't meant to last long. That's because the Ohlone moved from rich harvest to rich harvest, gathering seeds, salmon, and acorns.

So now I understand why their houses didn't look like teepees! They were more like modern-day tents.

Research is so important.

Love,

Penny

SUNDAY, MAY 3, 2015

Dear You,

A win in the first game of the Western Conference Semifinals! Dubs beat the Grizzlies 101–86! Woo-Hoo Zippity-Doo! Getting closer to the FINALS!!!!!

Love,

Penny

Dear You,

On Mondays after school, Hazel and Gabby and I race to Hazel's house to get the mail. Like streaks of lightning. Like the wind. Like the Warriors chasing the ball. Those are SIMILES, You. A simile is like a metaphor, but with the word *like* in front of it.

We need those similes on Mondays, because that's the day Rick has his appointment with his gum doctor. He comes home early to swish his mouth with warm salt water and then lie down. So the Splash Sisters race like Warriors and lightning and the wind and comets to get the mail before Rick gets home.

Anyway, nothing has come for me yet c/o Hazel in the mail.

When Rick came home, he poked his head in the room to yell at Hazel for not unloading the dishwasher. He is such a crabby man! I know he has sore gums and I should give him the benefit of the doubt, but I don't think it's only his gums.

Gabby: "When's he going to tell us about those Warriors tickets?"

Hazel just shrugged her shoulders.

It must be hard to live with that crabbiness. It would be like swishing salty water in your mouth all the time. Maybe Rick has a lot of important friends, but it's hard for me to imagine him having any friends at all.

Love,

Penny

PS. Sundae Monday flavor: Chestnut Chocolate Cream. Excellent.

THURSDAY, MAY 7, 2015

Dear You,

Worrisome News:

Hazel told us that a lonely widow came by to meet Nell. The woman has a few goats of her own. She said the widow was "very taken with Nell." And Hazel was quite concerned because Nell nuzzled the woman's hair. Hazel gave the woman information about Nell's unpleasant health problems.

And here is some very disappointing news:

Hazel also told me there is a chance she may be going out of town for my birthday celebration!

Couldn't her family postpone her trip for just one measly but important day? Gabby said that's what she'd make her family do, absolutely.

I don't understand.

Love,

Pen

Saturday, May 9: We lost game three, 89–99! Series is 2–1 in favor of the Grizzlies!!!

SUNDAY, MAY 10, 2015

Dear You,

Now I understand why Hazel can't come to my birthday party. I think.

Hazel admitted she fabricated. Her family is not going out of town. The real reason is that she is afraid Nell will be given away when she's at my party.

I told her she should have trusted me to understand.

Love,

Penny

TUESDAY, MAY 12, 2015

Dear You,

GOOD NEWS: Yesterday, the Warriors beat the Grizzlies in game four, 101–84, and they weren't even playing at home! The series is even now! Curry played like the MVP he is: He scored thirty-three points and got eight rebounds and five assists. His slump is over!

MORE GOOD NEWS. I think. Hazel can come to the museum (but not the sleepover). Her mom and Rick promised that nothing would happen with Nell while she's gone. But Hazel can't come for the sleepover, because she wants to spend every spare moment with Nell.

Gabby: "That's ridiculous. You don't SLEEP with your goat, and nobody will take her away in the dead of night."

Hazel: "Well, we're also having out-of-town guests, and it would be rude of me not to be there at all."

Anyway, at least she can come to the museum.

Love,

Penny

Happy Andrew Bogut Day, once again.

THURSDAY, MAY 14, 2015

Dear You,

There were rain showers today. Very unusual for the month of May! I hope that isn't a bad sign for the Dubs, I said to Mama. Even though they crushed the Grizzlies last night, 98–78, and are ahead in the series, 3–2.

No, Mama said, the rain is a sign of the effects of climate change. Mama thinks my superstitious thinking is because of anxiety. I think she's right. I wish I could tell Mama and Sammy that I am upset about my fabricated presentation in the auditorium without them there to cheer me on and be proud of me. And I'm worried that they will somehow find out I haven't invited them.

I am also worried about Nell. The lonely widow returned for a second meeting. Nell has a problem getting along with other goats, Hazel told her. She bites and butts ferociously. The woman said she would consider that in her final decision.

You are almost twenty-eight weeks old and approximately sixteen inches long. You have grown so much from that little speck you used to be. Will you end up being taller than me one day?

Love,
Me

FRIDAY, MAY 15, 2015

Dear You,

We went out for Mama's birthday dinner today at her favorite place, Fentons. Just me, Sammy, and Mama.

I gave Mama a homemade card and a giant box of chocolate turtles. I was hoping to give her some information about her long-lost relatives. I should say OUR long-lost relatives, You. I have received nothing from the Doppel Country Cousins Trio or the jam maker yet.

But Mama loved the turtles.

Tonight is the eve of my own birthday.

Mama told me that when I was born, she could tell I was relieved, because I yelled at her almost right away, as if I was finally able to complain about being cooped up for nine months.

Do you feel the same way, You?

Love,

Me, just about eleven

> Tonight, the Dubs beat the Grizzlies, 108–95 to win the series 4–2, and now they are off to the Western Conference Finals!!!!! Steph sunk a sixty-two-footer in the third quarter!!!!

SUNDAY, MAY 17, 2015

Dear You,

Well,

I'm Eleven.

DISAPPOINTED ADMISSION: My birthday was bittersweet, I am so sorry to say. I am only admitting this to you. I don't want to hurt Mama's or Sammy's feelings.

There was ONE OUTSTANDING SWEET EXPERIENCE and ONE OUTSTANDING BITTER EXPERIENCE.

Sammy drove the van to the museum because there were so many of us: me and my parents, Hazel, Gabby, and Angel. And Mele Lorraine and Mele Grace. Uncle Ziggy was troubadoring at a Thai restaurant and couldn't make it.

There were actually quite a few positive experiences at the museum. All of California's history, happy and sad, is in one big space. Native Americans, the Spanish, the Gold Rush, the Great Depression, the World Wars, Japanese internment camps, Cesar Chavez, Hollywood! So much to see and think about! I tried not to go through the different sections too quickly. It was interesting, but it all made my head spin.

And here was my OUTSTANDING SWEET EXPERIENCE:

Just about the very first thing you see when you walk into the museum is the beautiful Ohlone basket, protected under a glass case. It is at the beginning of all the exhibits, as if the basket is the beginning of the whole world itself.

It is not an original Ohlone basket. It is a replica

made by a talented Ohlone woman named Linda Yamane. REPLICA means copy. She did a lot of research. And she made it with the same materials the ancient Ohlone used.

There it was, created from pieces of the earth and the ocean and the sky, just as Mele Grace remembered it!

Hundreds and hundreds of stitches made of plant material were woven and knotted into coils. Black triangles of fern root made a pattern all around. Feathers from a red-winged blackbird and a mallard duck and the crest of a quail were also attached. And abalone beads hung from the coils like tiny stars.

But really, a thousand words can't describe how beautiful it is.

Mele Lorraine and Mele Grace were VERY teary, even though they had seen it before many times. Hazel sketched a picture of it.

Meanwhile, Angel had decided to hide inside a replica of an old beat-up car supposedly from the Midwest during the Depression, that terrible time in the 1930s when farms were drying up during a drought. The car had the sign CALIFORNIA OR BUST! hanging from the side of it. It took us thirty whole minutes to find her, and then she kept yelling, "Angel or Bust! Angel or Bust!" in a singsong voice, almost all the way home.

That was annoying, but it wasn't the outstanding bitter experience. That comes next.

LATER

It hurts so much to write about it. But I have to.

When we drove up to Hazel's house to drop her off, Rick and Hazel's mom were sitting on the outside steps. Liza gave us a lips-only smile and Rick just stared. Hazel leaped from the car.

Mama leaned out the window and shouted, "Enjoy your out-of-town guests!"

Rick frowned and looked at Hazel.

Rick: "What out-of-town guests?"

Mama: "The ones Hazel mentioned. Otherwise, we'd love her to join us now for pizza and a sleepover."

Rick: "No out-of-town guests planned. She just wanted to stay home with us, and we wanted her here, too."

Hazel's cheeks turned Petunia Pink. She ran inside her house.

So they weren't excuses. And they weren't reasons. They were just more fabrications.

I, a fabricator, shouldn't judge another fabricator. But Hazel's lie still hurt.

"Hazel wants to spend every spare second she has with her goat," I explained to Mama and Sammy.

But I don't really think that was the real reason.

Like Gabby said, she doesn't SLEEP with that goat.

What was the other reason?

I saw Mama and Sammy looking at each other as if they were reading each other's mind. I think I was thinking the same thing. I hope we are all wrong.

Love,

Me

MONDAY, MAY 18, 2015

Dear You,

Hazel wasn't in school today.

Just before dinnertime, Sammy answered the phone.

Sammy: "You're kidding me! No, she's not here."

It was Hazel's mom. She had stayed home from work because Hazel insisted on being with Nell on Nell's last day with the family. The lonely widow was arriving to pick up Nell that very evening. Hazel's scare tactics about Nell's indigestion and bowel and behavior problems just hadn't scared the widow away. Her mom said Hazel had gone out to the backyard this afternoon but she wasn't there anymore.

AND NELL WAS GONE, TOO!

Hazel's mom was telephoning us from her car because she and Rick were driving around the neighborhood, frantic with worry. Hazel and Nell were nowhere to be seen.

Me: "I think I know where they are."

And I was right. Because where else could they have been?

As Sammy and I turned the corner onto Hazel's street, we could see a telltale trail of poop drops leading to the stairway entrance. And all we could hear was "M-AH-AH-AH-AH!" coming from behind the garbage pails.

The Secret Stairway was no longer an ironclad secret. Neighbors were peering out their windows. Some were standing on the sidewalks. Behind the garbage pails, we found Hazel hugging Nell, Hazel's mouth a determined straight line, her eyes like slits.

Nell: "M-AH-AH-AH-AH!"

Way at the top of the secret stairs, leaning over the rickety fence, was a man and a woman and a little boy.

Man: "We kept asking what was wrong, but she wouldn't tell us."

Woman: "We were just about to call the authorities."

Boy: "Can we keep the goat? Can we keep the goat?"

Can we keep the goat.

That was what made Hazel's determined look crumple up. She began to cry.

Sammy: "Sweetie, your mom is very worried about you. I don't think Nell's a happy camper, either."

Nell: "M-AH-AH-AH-AH!"

Hazel must have known that the Time Had Come. Slowly, she stood up. She led Nell down the stairs by the leash attached to the goat's collar. What else could Hazel do? She'd tried everything.

Sammy, Hazel, and I slowly walked back down the street to Hazel's house, with Nell and her poop drops following behind. Hazel's mom and Rick (the goatist!) were pulling up in their car just as a woman driving a pickup truck was arriving, too.

It was the lonely widow in the pickup truck, a kindly looking little person with pink, apple-shaped cheeks. Under ordinary circumstances, I would find that fact amusing, because her name was Mrs. Applebaum. But nothing was amusing at that moment, and it's not even amusing now.

Hazel's mom hugged Hazel. But all Hazel wanted to do was hug Nell. Me, too. We put our arms around Nell's warm neck. We buried our noses in Nell's soft ears.

Nell: "M-AH-AH-AH-AH!"

Nell knew something was up. Nosiree, she didn't want to be separated from her family and friends! I began to feel hopeful. A little apple-cheeked person can't get a big, strong, stubborn goat to do what the goat doesn't want to do, I was thinking.

But Mrs. Applebaum knew her Nubian goats. She offered Nell some grain from the palm of her hand. Before we knew it, Nell allowed herself to be led to the pickup. Little Mrs. Applebaum, murmuring sweet nothings, quickly and expertly placed Nell's front legs onto the bumper and leaned on Nell's haunches. Then she moved Nell's head toward the truck to show her that there was even more grain inside.

And poor, hoodwinked Nell jumped right in! Mrs. Applebaum clanged shut the back of the pick-up and drove off.

It was all over. The goatist lit a cigarette. Hazel's mom put her arm around Hazel, who wasn't crying anymore. I guess she had emptied out all her tears and was kind of in shock.

Hazel's mom, to us: "Thank you so much for bringing my daughter home."

And she and the goatist and Hazel went inside their house. Sammy and I went home.

It was all so sad.

Love,

Penny

SUNDAY, MAY 24, 2015

Dear You,

There is so much to write, and I keep putting it off, but here goes.

SECRETS of the SECRET STAIRWAY (SOSS)
ANGRY FAREWELL EDITION

Yes, FAREWELL, I am sorry to say.

Hazel wasn't in school on Tuesday, either. But on Tuesday afternoon, she phoned both of us after school and asked us to please meet her at the Secret Stairway that afternoon.

Hazel gave both Gabby and me a small portrait of Nell. She had used watercolors and acrylics. They are beautiful and look just like Nell. Some people probably think all Nubian goats look alike, but those of us who know and love her can tell that it couldn't be any other goat but Nell.

Hazel: "I have to confess a few things. I want to apologize for getting your hopes up about going to a Warriors game. Rick never promised to take us. I lied. I just wanted you both to be my friends."

Gabby and I were very understanding at first. But I wasn't really surprised that she'd lied. As I said, it takes a fabricator to sniff out another one.

Gabby: "You were a new girl. I guess you really wanted to make friends."

Me: "I know what it's like to lie about something you want very much."

Hazel: "Thank you for understanding. I hate Rick with all my heart and soul. And Penny, I also want to confess something about your birthday sleepover. It wasn't me. It was Rick, mostly!"

Me: "What do you mean?"

Hazel: "I wanted to go to the sleepover at your house. But Rick and my mom wouldn't let me."

Me: "Why not?" (I already suspected the answer, You.)

Hazel: "Well, you know."

Me: "Not really." (I sort of did.)

Hazel: "Because you have two moms. Rick and my mom don't think that's right. They didn't want me staying overnight at your house. It's mostly Rick, though."

Me: "Why isn't it right to have two moms?"

Hazel: "Well, you know."

Me: "Actually, I don't."

Hazel wouldn't look at me: "Rick said it's just not right."

Me: "You said that already."

Hazel: "Rick didn't want me to go to the sleepover at Gabby's, either."

Gabby: "Why not?" (Of course, we knew the answer to that, too.)

Hazel: "Because he's a racist. My mom said I could go. But Rick put his foot down for YOUR sleepover,

Penny. He said he would move to Colorado without us if she allowed me to go to your party at a house with two moms."

Gabby, in her loud voice, the loud voice that everyone except her best friend (me) is surprised she has: "SO YOU SHOULD HAVE TOLD HIM TO MOVE TO COLORADO WITHOUT YOU!!!!!"

I agreed. I told her she should have stomped down hard, right on Rick's big feet! Or gone on a hunger strike. And told him what was right about my family.

Hazel just sat there with her head down, looking at her knuckles in her lap. And then Gabby and I got up and left the Secret Stairway, probably forever.

I am angry at Rick and Liza. I am angry at Hazel.

But I am also angry at MYSELF.

Because I didn't say everything I should have to Hazel. I didn't tell her what is very, very RIGHT about Mama and Sammy being together.

I should have told Hazel how happy they are and how much they love each other. How they are never crabby without apologizing right after, how they sing together, and how they read each other's mind, how they both cook our favorite foods and have Sundae Mondays and laugh at each other's dumb jokes, and how Mama brings Sammy ginger-mint tea when Sammy is working late, and how Sammy tucks a pillow behind Mama's back when it hurts, and how they take care of me as a team when I'm sick, and also when I'm not, and how they can't wait to have a baby in the house, and how they never, ever forget a birthday or an anniversary or a Valentine's Day or a Just-Something-to-Celebrate-Day, even if the cards are homemade. I wish I had said all that and much, much, much more.

I told Mama and Sammy what happened. They said there will be lots of times in my life when I will wish I'd said something when it is too late. That happens to everyone. But they are glad I wrote it all down.

Me, too.

For the record, even though it doesn't seem so important now: Last night, the Warriors beat Houston in their third game in the Western Conference Finals. 115–80. I have been watching the games, just not writing about them.

Love,

Penny

Dear You,

Gabby and I are not speaking to Hazel. We don't look at her disdainfully. We look at her sadly and with great disappointment in our eyes. Well, in Gabby's eyes, because I can't see my own eyes, but I'm sure they look just as hurt.

I thought I would want to be Hazel's friend forever.

Mama and Sammy say maybe I am being too hard on Hazel. And I say Hazel should have defended my family to her family!

I am learning that it is much easier to tell you happy things than not-so-happy things.

You are almost thirty weeks old now. I read in *What to Expect* that your brain is growing. It now has wrinkles and grooves so that it can expand even more later on. You are getting set "for a lifetime of learning."

So I guess my own brain has expanded a little. Because I have to tell you that a person realizes certain mature things when she moves further up in the double digits. This is what I have learned this week: People can disappoint you. A friendship can disappear—POOF!—just like that.

As Mama and Sammy always say, real life is harder than losing a basketball game. And there are more important things than winning one. Real life is not a GAME. I always knew that in my head. But I guess I never really felt it in my heart, deep down.

Sorry that I have to tell you all this, You.

The Warriors lost to Houston on Monday, 115–128.

And guess what? SO WHAT?

And then the Warriors beat the Rockets 104–90 tonight to close out the series. They are off to the NBA Finals against Cleveland.

That's nice, but guess what? SO WHAT?

Love,

Pen

PS. Hazel put a note in my mailbox. She said she is hoping against hope that I will find it in my heart to forgive her. She has thought about things and, of course, she knows my family is just as right as any other family. She just didn't have the words to say that to Rick.

She should have tried harder to find those words.

Except . . . even I didn't have the words for Hazel right away. So how could I expect Hazel to say them to Rick?

THURSDAY, MAY 28, 2015

Dear You,

Lots more has happened.

Momentous, soul-shattering things.

Remember Barbara Wolney, the jam maker, from Junoville, Wyoming?

She mailed a package to Hazel's address. Tonight, Hazel's mom brought it over.

Hazel's mom: "Rick wanted to mail it, but I thought it would be easier if I just brought it over."

Mama and Sammy looked puzzled. Of course, I knew immediately what it was.

Hazel's mom didn't stay very long, but she was very nice, thanking Mama and Sammy for taking Hazel to the museum. I wondered if Hazel had said anything to her.

It was a big box wrapped in brown paper. The return address said BARBARA WOLNEY, FRUIT OF THE VINE. The package was addressed to PENELOPE VICTORIA BACH, care of HAZEL PEPPER, with Hazel's address underneath that. Someone (probably Rick) had made a big, black, angry cross-out over that address and written PLEASE FORWARD, then scribbled our address instead.

Me: "Oh, I can explain what that is."

So I told them the whole story about using Hazel's iPad. And I said of course it was wrong to write to strangers on the Internet, but I was trying to track down clues about Mama's relatives as a surprise. And that I was still waiting for something from the Doppel Country Cousins Trio, which will probably be forwarded, too, if the Trio answers me.

"Wolney," Mama whispered. Her eyes were teary. I figured she was crying because of me writing to strangers on the Internet. Or maybe because I was having so much trouble tracking down relatives for her.

Sammy said, "Well, we may as well go ahead and open it."

So I tore off the brown paper, and underneath, there was a box wrapped in fancy paper decorated with balloons and cakes and candles and HAPPY BIRTHDAY written all over it. I didn't remember telling anyone about my birthday, I thought. I tore off the fancy paper and opened the box.

Inside were three big jars of gooseberry jam with labels that said FRESH FROM THE VINE.

And a little beige book called *poems of hooves and the wind in my hair*, by someone named Alfred J. Wolney.

And, also, a folded-up letter.

Me: "How come a stranger knows it's my birthday?"

Sammy opened the letter. Two photographs fell to the floor. Mama picked them up and looked at them. Tears poured out even more, as if they'd been hiding behind her eyes for a long time. She leaned her head on Sammy's shoulder and made Sammy's baby-blue T-shirt turn navy.

Sammy quickly glanced over the letter, then handed it to me.

Sammy was crying, too.

Dear Penelope,

My cousin, Barbara Wolney, the jam maker, gave me your letter.

My name is Al Wolney, a poet and also an accountant. A lover of both words and numbers, one would say.

I am also your grandfather.

Happy birthday!

Of course a grandfather knows his granddaughter's birth date! I am so happy you found me. I have been looking for you. I've never known where you lived, Penelope, since your mom changed both of your last names.

I wasn't going to tell you the truth about who I am. But I've changed my mind.

It has been almost nine years, and this old guy has learned a few things, and grown a bit, especially after my wife (and your grandmother), Carol, died. Say hello to your mother and Samantha. Tell them we were wrong, and that I am sorry. I hope they will find it in their hearts to forgive me, and that you will, too. They will explain what happened.

Please keep in touch. There are some pretty cool aunts and uncles and young cousins who want to meet you all.

Love,

Al Wolney

AJW@hoovesnwind.com

Turns out, Mama and Sammy told me, this Mr. Alfred J. Wolney, the locally famous Junoville poet, is MY relative, not Mama's. Turns out he is my dad's father! Turns out that, no, Mama doesn't have any relatives left in Junoville. She is an orphan, brought up in foster families, but my dad really wasn't an orphan.

Then Mama and Sammy told me a story I never knew until THIS VERY DAY.

Here it is:

When I was a very little, Mama and Sammy and I flew from California all the way to Wyoming to visit my dad's father, Al, and my dad's mother, Carol, who is now dead. They wanted to introduce them to their granddaughter.

Me.

We stayed in a hotel. Al and Carol invited the three of us to their home, but just for an afternoon visit. Mama and Sammy could smell chicken roasting in the kitchen, but we weren't asked to stay for dinner. That's because Al and Carol said they didn't think our family was "right," same as Liza and Rick don't.

So Mama and Sammy and I went home to California the next day, and they never spoke to Al and Carol again.

Mama picked up the photos that had fallen to the floor. She held up one of her and my dad on a motorcycle. A man was standing beside them with his hand on my dad's shoulder.

Mama: "That's your grandfather Al. It was taken by your grandmother Carol, just before your dad and I left for Oakland."

Then she held up another photo of a big brown horse. Al's horse, Belle, she said. But my dad rode her, too, from the time he was a boy.

Mama: "Of course, Belle must have died by now."

Mama put the photos against her heart, then in her lap.

But I felt anger like a volcano bubbling up inside of me because of the COLOSSAL HUGE GIGANTIC TREMENDOUS fabrication by my own parents, who never told me I had other relatives!!!!!!!!!! There are a hundred more synonyms I could have used, and they'd all mean BIGGER THAN BIG.

"You lied to me!" I said. Actually, I shouted.

My own parents created a fabrication for almost one whole decade!!!!!!!!!!!!!!! All my life, I had believed a romantic story about two orphans falling in love, and it was a big fat lie. They may have fallen in love, but only one of them was an orphan.

I am not speaking to Mama and Sammy at this point in time.

Love,

Pen

FRIDAY, MAY 29, 2015

Dear You,

I have only had a few tiny conversations with Mama and Sammy since last night. They have done almost all of the talking.

Mama: "Honey, we just didn't want you to get hurt. But adults don't always do the right thing, especially when they are hurting, too."

Sammy: "We made a big mistake. We tried to protect you too much."

Mama: "I am so sorry, sweetheart."

Sammy: "I hope you will forgive us one day. Everyone should know who her relatives are."

Me, to all that: SILENCE.

Mama, with a sheepish smile. And SHEEPISH has nothing to do with sheep, if you remember, You.

"Isn't it wonderful that of all the people in Junoville, your letter found its way to your own grandfather? Could it be some sort of sign?"

Me, because I couldn't help it: "There aren't THAT many people in Junoville, so it's not that amazing!!!! Anyway, I thought you said you didn't believe in signs and magical thinking and superstitions!"

Mama: "Well, maybe I'm starting to."

Me: "Hmmmf!!!!!"

Sammy: "Will you ever speak to us again? It's getting boring around here without your conversations and questions."

Me: SILENCE.

I have to admit that not talking to Mama and Sammy is harder than going on a hunger strike.

I told Gabby, and she was flabbergasted at what has happened. But she said she sort of understands how both sides feel. I'm not sure I do.

Love,

Penny

Oh, Mama.

Oh, You.

Please, please hold on to each other.

2 P.M.

Mama and Sammy have left for the hospital. Mama was having some contractions. You want to be born.

3 P.M.

It's too early for you to be born! You have some more growing to do. Just about two months' worth.

Uncle Ziggy is here, we are scared, and I'm so, so, so sorry.

9 P.M.

Why did I upset Mama by expressing my disappointment and by not having empathy?

Uncle Ziggy said it was ABSOLUTELY NOT my fault!

Love,

Penny

SUNDAY, MAY 31, 2015

Dear You,

Mama is coming home this afternoon. The contractions inside of her have stopped. You and she are fine so far. The doctors told her to rest in bed. You wanted to come a bit too early, but I guess you changed your mind.

1 P.M.

I AM SO RELIEVED!!!!!!!!!!!!!!!!!!!!!

Mama and you are home.

I think this has been my fault. Sammy says "ABSO-LUTELY NOT." She must have told me that forty-two times. Still, I don't believe her.

7 P.M.

I want to make a few vows.

I vow to take care of Mama as much as I can.

I will never yell at Mama again. Or Sammy.

And I have been spending much too much time scribbling in this journal and thinking about basketball, and, of course, fabricating. Winning isn't everything, and losing isn't the end of the world. That's what a mature person understands.

And if you will just hang on for a little while longer, You, I HEREBY MAKE A SOLEMN VOW TO BE A BETTER HUMAN BEING IN GENERAL. I VOW TO WORK INCREDIBLY HARD TO BE AN OLDER, MATURE SISTER YOU WILL BE PROUD OF. I WILL NO LONGER FABRICATE. I WILL EVEN TELL MR. CHEN THE TRUTH ABOUT MY DNA ASAP. I WILL EVEN STAND UP ON THAT STAGE IN THE AUDITORIUM AND CONFESS IN FRONT OF THE WHOLE SCHOOL!!!! AND, OF COURSE, CONFESS ALL TO MAMA AND SAMMY.

If you will only, only continue to hold on, You.

We will meet again in person after you are born.

Meanwhile, I will be busy helping Sammy around the house, making sure Mama rests, concentrating hard on being mature, and building up my courage to tell the truth.

So until you are born,

Farewell,
Farewell ((♡))

Love,
Penelope

Dear You,

Hello, I'm back.

Yesterday, Mama said she couldn't stand me slouching around the house with a long face, staring at her with big, mopey eyes. I told her I just wanted to help out. I have been racing home after school every day. Mama stays on the couch most of the time. The days are very warm, so Sammy plugged in a fan that slowly blows cool air on Mama's perspiring face. Sammy and I bring her trays of sandwiches and cold lemonade.

Mama: "Do you want to know how you can help out?"

Me: "How?"

Mama: "You can do three things."

Me: "Sure, anything!!!!!!!!!!!!!!"

Mama: "NUMBER ONE: Go outside and shoot hoops with Gabby. Every day. NUMBER TWO: Get back to your journal. Writing makes you feel better. NUMBER THREE: Watch the NBA Finals against Cleveland with Sammy and me. You can educate us about basketball and how to be great Warriors fans."

Three easy things. Three things I would love to do. Three things that feel like three gifts I really don't deserve.

I began their education right away. We watched game one together in bed with Mama last night.

Then I gave them homework. Actually, it was a quiz. I gave them permission to use YouTube if they were stumped.

Love,

Pen

QUIZ FOR MAMA AND SAMMY
JUNE 4, 2015, GAME ONE, NBA FINALS V
CLEVELAND CAVALIERS

I am beginning your quiz with an easy question.

1. Who won and what was the score?
2. Who is the Cavs' star player and how many points did he score?
3. Why does everyone hate LeBron James?
4. Which team had the most rebounds?
5. Which Warrior had a concussion in his last game but was able to score twenty-one points?
6. Who cheered the loudest in our house?

SATURDAY, JUNE 6, 2015

Dear You,

Mama and Sammy did well on their quiz except for #3. They said that they couldn't understand why everyone is so enraged at the Cavs' LeBron James, just because he is such a good player.

They are recent fans, so I had to explain about LeBron being a traitor to the Cavs and leaving them for the Heat and how heartbroken the Cavs fans had been. And how even though he returned to them, many people still can't forgive him.

Sammy says that HATE and TRAITOR and HEART-BROKEN are very strong words to use when talking about a basketball game, but I certainly don't agree.

Love,

Penny

SUNDAY, JUNE 7, 2015

Dear You,

While I was not speaking to Mama and Sammy, they were busy speaking to Al Wolney. They emailed him. Then they phoned him. I was flabbergasted. They told me they wanted to make amends to both him and me, if it wasn't too late.

So guess what? This afternoon we all Skyped him.

Mama: "You look well, Al."

Al: "You and Samantha look exactly the same! But who is that young lady with you?"

Me: "I'm Penelope."

Duh.

Al: "You mentioned that we don't have a professional basketball team out here. True, but I like the game. I would really enjoy talking basketball with you some time."

Me: "Sure."

I was too shy to look him in the eye. But when you Skype someone, you are supposed to look at the tiny camera hole at the top of the computer. The other person thinks you are looking straight at him, but you really aren't.

I did take a quick peek at him.

Al has a big gray beard and kind eyes and a giant smile. He has much, much less hair on his head than in the old photo he sent of himself and my parents. So I guess the wind in his hair in his book title happened a long time ago. I think I saw a gap between his front two teeth, like my dad's.

He still seemed like a stranger, though. Not a grandfather.

After we'd all chatted a bit more and said goodbye,

I asked Mama and Sammy why they'd forgiven Al. Mama said that the great thing about forgiveness is that the forgiver feels just as good as the forgiven.

Sammy: "People learn and change. Look at us! We're basketball fans now."

Mama: "And by the way, are WE forgiven?"

Me: "Depends how you do on the next quiz."

Game two was a loss, 93–95. Mama and Sammy were just as disappointed as I was. But Mama and Sammy admitted that watching the game all the way through made everything more exciting.

Duh! It's about time they found that out.

Love,

Penny

PS. I am thinking about the people in my own life I haven't forgiven.

QUIZ FOR MAMA AND SAMMY
JUNE 7, 2015, GAME TWO, NBA FINALS V CLEVELAND CAVALIERS

1. Who won and what was the score?
2. For each team, which player had the most points?

3. Give the main reason why people didn't think the Cavs would win.
4. Who hit LeBron in the face in the fourth quarter?
5. How was this game similar to the end of game one?
6. Who made the last free throws of the game?

MONDAY, JUNE 8, 2015

Dear You,

What to Expect says you weigh over three pounds already. You are around eighteen inches.

Good for you, You.

I want you to know that I have grown up a little, too.

I have kept my vow.

It isn't easy to fix a lie. It's like untying a tight knot in a shoelace. Not that long ago, I used to get lots of knots in my shoelaces, because I wasn't used to tying bows. On account of all those sneakers with Velcro straps I wore when I was little.

But today after school, I told Mr. Chen I needed to talk to him about something important. I was nervous. My hands were shaking, so if I had a real knot to untie, I probably couldn't have done it.

Mr. Chen was at his desk. His summer tie had

a pale blue sky, a dark green ocean, and an empty golden beach with two bare feet sticking up. If you looked at it long enough, you could imagine yourself lying on that beach.

Here is his tie:

You may think I'm digressing. But I'm not. It was a hot day, and Mr. Chen's tie made me feel cooler and calmer. And so did his kind, kind eyes.

I just blurted everything out right away. I told him that the early Ohlone are not really my ancestors. They are Sammy's.

Me: "Sammy is my mother's domestic partner. She has adopted me, but we are not really related through DNA. I borrowed her heritage. I guess my imagination got carried away when I told you about it the first time."

"It happens," said Mr. Chen kindly.

But then I told him that it wasn't only my imagination. Because I knew darn well I'd been fabricating, and then I got stuck inside my fabricating and I couldn't climb out. Like sinking into a big muddy sinkhole.

And even the basket was a lie, because it only existed in Mele Grace's memory, I told him.

ME: "I did lots of research, though. It was all extremely interesting."

I showed Mr. Chen my poodle notebook with all my Ohlone notes and my drawings, copied from the books he'd lent me, from what I remembered from third grade, and from what I'd learned from Sammy and her relatives. I told him about the protests at the Bay Street mall.

He looked thoughtful, leafing through the pages of the notebook.

Me: "At this point in time I have some information about my Wyoming relatives. I can talk about them instead. But first, I want to confess my lie to the whole school."

Mr. Chen: "This is wonderful research, Penny. And I can tell how sorry you are. It seems to me you can still present your research about both sides of your family. I think the younger grades and their teachers would appreciate your personal experience with regards to what they are studying. You have some important things to share. And Sammy is your parent, after all."

Me: "I know she is."

Mr. Chen: "So go for it!"

I ran home because I couldn't wait to tell Mama and Sammy the whole story. They said they were mostly sorry I had been keeping everything inside all this time.

Well, no, I said. I told Gabby and Hazel, and I have been writing about it in my golden retriever journal. They were both very glad to hear that.

Mama: "But we should have told you the truth all along. Maybe that's why you felt you needed that story about your heritage. Big secrets can make a family sing off-key."

"That's a good use of metaphor, Mama," I said.

I liked her word *story* too, even though I knew *lie* was the better word.

Sammy: "And of course you should talk about my family's history in your presentation! But why do you have to say 'parent by domestic partnership'? Can't you drop a few words and just say 'parent'?"

Me: "Of course I can."

I love Sammy so much.

Love,

Penelope

LATER, BEFORE BED

Here is one of Mr. Al Wolney's poems. It doesn't rhyme, and I don't really understand it, but I like it. He uses his senses, which Mr. Chen says is a good thing to do when you write. Mr. Chen also says that, sometimes, you don't have to totally understand a poem to think it is beautiful.

Ah, Belle,
Daughter of Juno,
pounding hoof
kind eye
ear soft to my touch
sweet smell of hay
more precious now than then.

I guess he is saying he is awfully lonely since his horse and wife died. He didn't really say that in his letter, but he said it in his poem.

WHAT I LOVE TO TOUCH
Mama's belly
Flower petals

Warm water in the bath

A dog's nose

Mele Grace's cheek

TUESDAY, JUNE 9, 2015

Dear You,

Gabby and I walked over to Hazel's house after school. When we rang the doorbell, she opened the door right away, as if she had been waiting for us, even though we hadn't phoned in advance or anything. Maybe she had been looking out the window every day, hoping we'd come by.

I'm glad we did. She looked so happy to see us.

Hazel, talking very fast: "Penny, I have thought and thought about everything. I should have said something to Rick! Please don't think I agreed with him. I should have been a better friend. I was just so, so sad and mixed-up that week. Please accept my absolutely sincerest utmost apology."

Hazel said she still hated Rick, but she is trying to make the best of things. And the other day, Hazel's mother and Rick had a fight and Hazel's mom yelled at Rick to move back to Colorado. But Rick asked to stay. Hazel told him that if he stayed, he had to stop bossing her around, because he is not her father or her stepfather. And he had to try to stop smoking and work on his prejudices.

Rick has begun Smokenders Online. She is not sure if he is working on his prejudices.

Me: "Sometimes people learn and change."

Hazel: "Hope so. But will you please accept my apology?"

Me: "Yes, I accept it."

That is all we both needed to say. I thought it would be harder to repair a friendship gone wrong, but it was actually easy. And forgiveness really does feel good. Gabby forgave her, too.

Then Hazel asked her mother to phone Mrs. Applebaum and ask if we could visit Nell. Hazel said Mrs. Applebaum is always home and always says yes, and Hazel was right. Hazel's mom drove us over.

Mrs. Applebaum: "Welcome! I just happened to make some fresh yogurt from the goats' milk! Let's have it in the backyard with Nell."

Nell nuzzled our hair when we hugged her. You could tell she remembered all of us. And it made us happy to know that Nell has some goat buddies. Mrs. Applebaum says Nell gets along with all the other goats and seems to have overcome her biting and butting problem (hee-hee).

Nell: "M-AH-AH-AH-AH!"

We think she was saying, "I'M OK. DON'T WORRY!"

By the way, yogurt made from goat's milk must be an acquired taste. Hazel and her mom gobbled theirs down, but they had previously acquired a taste for it. Gabby and I are not sure we actually want to acquire a taste for it, but we ate some anyway. We will be visiting Nell pretty regularly, and we don't want to hurt nice Mrs. Applebaum's feelings.

Love,

Penelope

PS. I really wanted a win in game three, especially the night before my presentation, but we lost 91–96. I am trying to be mature and hopeful. But I began to worry that if the Dubs lost to the Cavs, then my presentation wouldn't go well. Sammy slapped her hand to her forehead and said my presentation has absolutely nothing to do with the game and everything will be fine. And to STOP being superstitious.

It did make me feel better about my presentation to yell at the Cavs on TV tonight.

QUIZ FOR MAMA AND SAMMY
JUNE 9, 2015, GAME THREE, NBA FINALS V.
CLEVELAND CAVALIERS

1. Who won and what was the score?
2. How many years has it been since Cleveland won a championship?
3. How many years has it been for the Warriors?
4. For each team, which player had the most points? The most assists?
5. How many points did the Dubs trail at the end of the third quarter?
6. How did Curry help to make that up?

WEDNESDAY, JUNE 10, 2015

Dear You,

The Ohlone believed that their dreams were important. A dream about a kindly hunting friend wishing them well before a dangerous hunting trip was a good sign.

Last night, I dreamed about Steph Curry. He said, "Go for it!" which was what Mr. Chen said to me, too.

So I did wake up this morning feeling better than I had last night.

Mama and Sammy were in the school auditorium, in the very first row. So were Mele Lorraine and Mele Grace. Uncle Ziggy videotaped the whole thing.

Everyone's presentation was very interesting. I wish I had time to describe them all.

Gabby showed slides of her grandparents' sugarcane farm in Jamaica. She held up some sugarcane samples that her mother bought in an Oakland market.

I really liked Amir's talk about Calcutta and his very special visual aid—his mom! She modeled her exquisite sari from the stage.

Mia's parents didn't move from very far away (L.A.), but we all enjoyed her cool photos of Universal Studios and her grandfather surfing in the ocean when he was a teenager.

Hazel talked about the royal family in London and also showed a photo of the Russian samovar, now a lamp, which once belonged to a czar's cousin.

Kenny's parents came to California from New York. He mentioned his dad's favorite basketball team, the Knicks. Some kids in the audience booed their heads off. Mr. Chen jumped up from his seat and held up his hand for silence. I've actually NEVER seen Mr. Chen look that angry!

Then Kenny told everyone that he had visited his dad

in the city of Camarillo to interview him. He said his dad was in the penitentiary there, but he is coming home pretty soon. It has been hard for everyone, he said.

I admit that Kenny showed brave maturity for telling that story.

When it was my turn to tell my own story, I wasn't as brave. My hands were clammy, especially because Mrs. Solomon, the principal, and some office staff trooped into the auditorium just before my talk.

Sammy had helped me set up her laptop for a slide presentation.

Mama had helped me figure out what to say. She advised me to have an opening statement and a big finish. I used index cards like she does in all of her talks.

As soon as I started to speak, I wasn't nervous anymore. (Mama had told me this would happen.)

MY OPENING STATEMENT:

"My biological heritage is from my parents Rebecca and William, who came to Oakland from Wyoming. But my dad died when I was very little. Sammy is my mom's domestic partner. She is part Ohlone. She adopted me. She is not a relative by DNA, as I once told my class. But she is a relative by LOVE. Love is just as important as DNA. Actually, more."

My voice wobbled a little when I said that last part.

I had to stop and take a big breath. Sammy winked at me.

Then I showed slides of the state of Wyoming, its shape an almost perfect rectangle. I showed photos of the Rocky Mountains, the High Plains, Grand Teton, and Yellowstone. I got most of my information from the Internet. I showed a slide of Belle, Al Wolney's horse, and another of my mom and dad on that motorcycle. I compared my parents to the long-ago explorers the fifth-graders are studying, bravely venturing to new vistas.

But a lot of my talk was about the Ohlone, how they built their houses, what food they ate, how they used their senses, and how they patiently took care of one another and everything on earth. And I talked about how they were forced to live in the California missions from the eighteenth century, and, sadly, made to forget the Ohlone ways.

Those were facts we had already learned in third grade and reviewed in other grades, but everyone was listening intently.

I also described how the Ohlone made woven baskets and how these baskets were both works of art and useful. Then I showed a slide of the Oakland Museum of California's replica of an Ohlone basket.

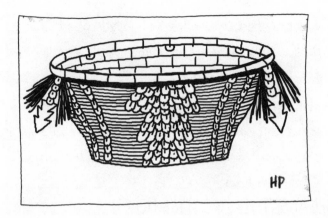

I told the audience that although Hazel Pepper's drawing was excellent, they should go to the museum to see the basket in real life. No drawing or even a thousand words can describe how beautiful it is, I said.

Finally, I talked about the Ohlone modern-day protests and prayer vigils to honor their ancestors at the little memorial park near the Bay Street mall in Emeryville. I showed a slide of the mall. I told the audience it was built on top of the sacred Ohlone remains. I said it was our duty to make sure that doesn't happen again, to anyone's ancestors.

Most of the kids didn't know those particular facts. I could tell by their shocked faces.

And then I gave MY BIG FINISH:

I am proud of it. Here are my last three index cards.

> The Ohlone share this land, which they love, with us.
>
> Actually, sadly, as you know, other people who came after stole their land away from them.
>
> So the East Bay was the home of Chochenyo Ohlone for thousands and thousands of years before it was ours. It is actually more the Ohlone's home than anybody's. But their story is not only about olden times.
>
> BECAUSE THEY ARE STILL HERE.

Then I said, "Now I'd like to introduce you to my mom, Sammy, my mele Lorraine, my mele Grace, and my uncle Ziggy, who are in the audience at this time. They are Ohlone. *Mele* means grandmother as well as great-grandmother in their native language, which is Chochenyo."

Sammy, Mele Lorraine, Mele Grace, and Uncle Ziggy stood up and turned around to wave at everyone. The audience clapped.

I continued:

> Now, this land is our home, too, and we are all related because of that. And we have to take care of our home like the Ohlone have always believed we should do. We also have to take care of one another, like a FAMILY does.

> How do we do all that?
>
> I will tell you.
>
> 1. By not causing pollution
>
> 2. By saving water and energy and respecting the earth's resources
>
> 3. By being kind, and having empathy, and being respectful of one another's differences, and loving one another.
>
> 4. By playing and watching SPORTS instead of having WARS that destroy everything!!!!!!!!!
>
> Thank you for listening, ladies and gentlemen, girls and boys!!!!!!

My presentation was longer than I'd expected. But I don't think it was boring, because everyone clapped very loudly, especially my family and Gabby. I saw Hazel giving me her special version of a thumbs-up with her upside-down, double-jointed thumb.

Later, Mr. Chen said my presentation was excellent and worth waiting for. And I told him that every word of it was true.

At our class party, we tasted pho and spaghetti and samosas and fried rice and Persian rice and sushi and cornbread and enchiladas and veggie burgers and matzo ball soup and jerk chicken (Gabby's) and börek and kebobs and kugel and flan and borsht (Hazel's) and English trifle (also Hazel's) and, well, MORE. And . . . Mele Grace's salad with manzanita berry dressing.

Love,

Penelope

THURSDAY, JUNE 11, 2015

Dear You,

Today was the last day of school. Off to middle school in the fall!

So much has happened this year.

Or does it just seem like a lot happened because I wrote it down?

Mr. Chen calls that a RHETORICAL QUESTION.

A question without an answer.

No, there is an answer.

A lot happened. And I wrote it down.

Love,

Penelope

PS. We all can't wait until game four tonight!

QUIZ FOR MAMA AND SAMMY
JUNE 11, 2015, GAME FOUR, NBA FINALS V
CLEVELAND CAVALIERS

1. Who won and what was the score?

2. Why did the Dubs HAVE TO win this game?

3. Who was in the starting lineup for the first time this season?

4. What did he do that was so great?

SATURDAY, JUNE 13, 2015

Dear You,

Mama says she feels healthy and strong. She rests a lot. You are kicking and moving as if you were revving up to be born. Sammy is cooking and freezing meals for when you arrive because nobody will have much time to cook. Our house is quiet and peaceful. We don't do too much, really, except watch TV, talk about basketball, play board games, and eat.

Mama says it's the calm before the storm, and you are the storm. A good storm, like the rain we hoped for all year.

Here you are now:

Love,

Penelope

Dear You,

I can't believe I just wrote that! Uncle Ziggy bought a bunch of tickets to celebrate my graduation!

Even though Mama and Sammy are Fans-in-Training, we agreed that Gabby and Hazel should go with me as fellow graduates and supremely loyal and longstanding Dubs fans.

Uncle Ziggy picked us up early so we could watch Steph warming up. We were all wearing our yellow Warriors tees.

When we picked up Gabby, Angel ran out to the car, too, a homemade DUBS OR BUST sign pinned to her T-shirt, crying her head off. Her dad had to pick her up to calm her down. I had empathy for her. I will have empathy for you, too, You. It is hard to be little and miss out on so many things.

After we'd parked, we walked the long, long bridge to the stadium with hundreds of other excited people. The Oracle looks like a huge ship lighting up the night.

And inside! A sea of yellow shirts and blue shirts. Everyone talking and yelling! The smell of the fries. The taste of my hot dog. My very own ticket burning up my hand. Yesiree, all of my senses were working like crazy.

We found our seats, and soon the Cavs came onto the court, then the Dubs. Gabby and Hazel and I sat in frozen silence, watching them warm up. I couldn't believe I was BREATHING THE SAME AIR in the same big arena as our team!

As soon as the game started, Gabby and Hazel and I weren't frozen in silence anymore. We didn't need to follow the instructions on the big sign flashing CHEER MAKE NOISE. We were already doing that, nonstop.

I will use two words to describe this game.

Steph. Curry.

He made seven three-pointers and scored thirty-seven points and got seven rebounds and four assists.

He did that move we love, losing the Cavs' Matthew Dellavedova late in the fourth quarter, dribbling behind his back, crossing over, then shooting a three. So great to see his great moves in person!

But I am not being fair. Everyone was great.

Before Curry's shot, LeBron James made a thirty-four-footer that cut the Warriors' lead to only one point. We were scared for our team, but we couldn't help being in AWE. I was surprised to find out that I didn't hate him as much, seeing him in person, even though he'd been a traitor. After all, he is somebody's father. I saw him and his kids on TV. And he made basketball look so beautiful. He was carrying the whole team on his back, Uncle Ziggy said.

But our Warriors just kept making those three-pointers! And Andre Iguodala shot a three and then made a trick shot. He grabbed the rebound and tossed it in with his left hand!

After that, Steph Curry's three-pointers just kept coming. When Steph Curry had the ball, the basket seemed as wide as a swimming pool. He made every shot look easy.

And did I say we won the game? We did! 104–91.

WAIT! One more thing happened!

We looked up at the humongous jumbotron, and guess who was on it, singing War-ri-ors, War-ri-ors! and dancing to the music?

The Three OF US!

Love,
Penelope

PS. Proof that Mama and Sammy watched the game, even though I wasn't with them: THEY SAW US ON THE JUMBOTRON! I decided their reward was no quiz for game five.

TUESDAY, JUNE 16, 2015

Dear You,

Uncle Ziggy was wearing his stinky socks (and probably stinky underwear, too). Mama had slept in her Warriors hat the night before. Sammy kept her fingers crossed all through the game, even when she drank her iced tea. And I didn't let go of my lucky plastic four-leaf clover.

I guess it all worked!

Love,

Penelope

QUIZ FOR MAMA AND SAMMY
JUNE 16, 2015, GAME SIX, NBA FINALS V
CLEVELAND CAVALIERS

1. Who won and what was the score?
2. Who are now the NBA CHAMPIONS?
3. Which Warriors made those three-pointers in the fourth quarter?
4. Who is the NBA Finals MVP?
5. Who are the NBA CHAMPIONS?!!!
6. WHO ARE THE NBA CHAMPIONS?!!!

FRIDAY, JUNE 19, 2015

Dear You,

I am staying up late to write this because I want to get it all down right away. Today was the Oakland victory parade for the Warriors!

It felt as if a million people were there. And guess what? There were MORE than a million people at the parade and the rally! We heard that fact later on TV.

Sammy and Uncle Ziggy and I were lined up near Oakland Cathedral on Harrison Street early, way before nine. Mama stayed home, of course, but she watched the parade on TV.

The sky was deep, deep blue. Everyone was cheering and crammed tightly together. Car horns were honking. Confetti was flying like blue-and-gold snowflakes. I saw a man with a cobra around his neck. I saw a lady walking with a Shetland pony. I saw Go Dubs painted everywhere—on cars, on signs, and on people's faces.

Uncle Ziggy said some San Francisco big shots wanted to have the parade in that city. But Oakland said, NOSIREE—we want this parade! This is OUR beautiful day in OUR beautiful city and no one can take it away from us! WE are the Dub Nation! Oakland is THE city now! Take THAT, San Francisco!

I think every city should have a parade. A peaceful parade with no arguing or fighting. A happy parade where everybody's family came from a different place in the world once upon a time, but here we all are in the same city, feeling proud. A fun parade with floats that make you stop thinking only about yourself and your problems and the things in the world that scare you.

And a parade that shows how good your city is deep down, even though some people in other cities may think their cities are better. Like the Warriors! Their loyal fans knew how great they could be for forty long years when they were losing. Look at them now!

Even the police were like all the rest of us, just plain old fans who were happy and proud. Except they were wearing uniforms, of course. I looked for the cop who stopped Mike. I didn't see him. Maybe he doesn't care about the Warriors.

Anyway, I'm glad I didn't see him.

When Steph Curry's float rounded the corner, he was shouting at his fans and holding up the big Larry O'Brien Championship Trophy. He almost fell off! As the Warriors floated by us, they read our minds and we read theirs.

Us: "Thank you!"

The Dubs: "It was our pleasure."

Then we went home to watch the Warriors on TV like we usually do, even though we had just seen them in person. There was a giant rally outside the Henry J. Kaiser Convention Center near the lake, waiting for the Warriors' speeches.

Little Riley Curry, Steph Curry's daughter, was up on the stage.

MVT. Most Valuable Toddler.

Sammy told us that Fairyland was renamed Riley-land for the day.

I bet every kid wondered what it is like to be Steph Curry's child. Maybe even feeling a tiny bit jealous, and that's only natural.

All the speeches were wonderful.

Our mayor, Libby Schaff, said, "This city has had a love affair with this team!"

Steph Curry: "We're going to suit up in three months and try to do it again next year!"

Me and Uncle Ziggy and Mama and Sammy: "YES, WE CAN!"

Love,

Penelope

SATURDAY, JUNE 20, 2015

Dear You,

I was waiting for Gabby, making shots in her drive-way. Mike came outside. He watched me make a bunch of baskets in a row, using his cookie-jar tip.

"You're really good, Penny!" he said. "You should definitely play on a team."

That is one of the best compliments I've ever received in my life. Because it came from Mike.

I wanted to tell Mike that he should coach us now. But I was too shy. And then, of course, I remembered that we didn't even have a team.

Love,

Penelope

SUNDAY, JUNE 21, 2015

Dear You,

This morning Gabby phoned and said that Mike had a surprise for us and would be picking up Hazel and me in an hour.

Lee-Anne was in the front seat. She said she knew what the surprise was, but she wasn't telling. We would find out when we got there, except she didn't tell us where THERE was.

We picked up Hazel, and before I knew it, we were pulling up to the high school. We all got out and trooped into the high school gym.

Lee-Anne: "Gabby told me about that list of names on the bulletin board at your school. I wish I'd known you were looking for a league to play in. You really didn't have to wait this long! I know some girls' leagues. I can help you get set up to play this summer."

Gabby and Hazel and I hoorayed our heads off.

"And," said Lee-Anne, "you are looking at your new coach."

More hooraying!

Lee-Anne: "OK, listen up, gals. You are awesome, and it will be an awesome team, but I warn you—I'm tough."

Lee-Anne sure doesn't look tough, I thought. Tough doesn't smell like peppermint and roses.

But I was wrong! First, we stretched. Then she made us sprint around the court at different speeds. Then we did dribbling drills. And layup drills. And we finished practice with a 3 v 2 scrimmage, kids against adults. It was all hard work but so much fun. We sweated A LOT.

After that, we went to Fentons for lunch and ice cream, Lee-Anne and Mike's treat. Mike looked very happy. I realized I felt happy because Mike was happy. So I do feel true love for him after all, even though Lee-Anne is his girlfriend and not me.

Time has healed.

And there was one more surprise!

Mike drove us all to the Oakland Museum of California. Right off the entrance to the Gallery of California History was a small room totally filled with GOLDEN STATE WARRIORS STUFF!

There were autographed basketballs and a jersey signed by all the players and a 2015 championship ring. One wall had a life-size photo of the whole team.

But the best part was the basketball shoes, displayed in a big glass case. The actual shoes of Klay Thompson, Harrison Barnes, and Festus Ezeli! Those shoes were HUMONGOUS! It was hard to believe they were the real things and not fake.

Here is how they compared with my sneaker:

I kept thinking that in another room, right next door, people were peering at Linda Yamane's Ohlone basket, hushed and respectful and awestruck. And here we were, also hushed and respectful and awestruck, looking at those giant shoes. That probably means something important. I will certainly try to figure it out later.

Guess who else was in that little room?

Kenny Walinhoff and his mother. Kenny gave me a

little hello-there smile, then turned quickly away. Of course he had been expecting my deeply disdainful look, as usual.

I surprised him. And myself, too. I marched right over and put out my hand.

Me: "Hey, Kenny. Truce?"

Kenny (look of shock on face): "Uh, OK."

So we shook on it.

Kenny: "Hey, I saw you guys on the jumbotron at game five."

Me: "You did?"

And after that, we didn't know what else to say, but we were still shaking hands. It was very mature. And guess what? My heart fluttered.

Then Kenny finally said: "It's a good thing those giant shoes are behind glass, because—P.U.—they'd stink up the room!"

Which wasn't exactly mature, but I laughed my head off.

Wow, what a day.

Love,

Penelope

FRIDAY, JUNE 26, 2015

Dear You,

Today, Mama and Sammy were crying, but I knew they were crying tears of joy. People don't usually smile when they're crying

Mama said, "This is history in the making, Penny."

Her voice was shaking. "The Supreme Court has voted to end the ban of same-sex marriage across the nation."

Mama told me some of the history although I knew a lot of it already. Lawyers have been working toward this for years and years, state government by state government. Sometimes they won and sometimes they lost, but they kept on trying.

And today, they won in the highest court in the land.

There was dancing the streets. We watched it on TV tonight.

Sammy: "The joy for the Warriors' win last week and the joy tonight have the same source. The impossible was made possible."

And Mama said, "With much hard work and love and hope and a mighty team effort."

I will always remember this date,

June 26, 2015

when the impossible was made possible and everyone danced in the streets. But today the dancing in the streets was happening all over the world.

And then, all of a sudden, I knew EXACTLY why I wanted Mama and Sammy to get married, even though they had a domestic partnership and a marriage of the heart.

Me: "When the Dubs won the championship, everyone found out that Oakland is the City. Just as good as San Francisco! And if you get married, everyone will know our family is just as good as everyone else's."

Mama and Sammy stared at me. You could say that their mouths kind of dropped open. Then they looked at each other, read each other's minds, and said this, at the exact same time:

Mama to Sammy and Sammy to Mama: "WILL YOU MARRY ME?"

Mama to Sammy and Sammy to Mama: "YES!"

They both put their arms around me, and I started crying for joy, too. But also for some reasons I'm not really sure about.

Just to cry, I guess.

Love,

Penny

FRIDAY, JULY 3, 2015

Dear You,

MAMA AND SAMMY ARE PLANNING A WEDDING!

I am a little behind in my journal writing because I have been busy helping with wedding invitations and decorations and weeding and planting flowers in the backyard for the wedding.

Also, Grandpa Al Wolney is here! He rented a car and is helping us with errands—a great big help. We also went to Jack London Square and Fairyland and hiking and Fentons and farmers' markets. And, OK, an afternoon in San Francisco.

He is staying at our house and sleeping in the living room. I'm pretty confident I will love him soon. He's very kind.

But Grandpa Al and I still have more to learn about each other.

For instance, he gave me the *Rainbow Families Coloring Book*, which celebrates all kinds of families. He bought it at the San Francisco airport. I didn't tell him I am too old for a coloring book, or that I never really enjoyed coloring. I didn't want to hurt his feelings.

I will save it for you.

Love,

Penelope

TUESDAY, JULY 7, 2015

Dear Mary Joy,

THAT'S YOU!

YOU HAVE ARRIVED!!!!!!!!!!!!!!!!!!!!!!!!!!!!

(Oops, the Queen of Exclamation Points is doing it again. Can't help it!! !! !! !!!)

Your birth date was yesterday, MONDAY, JULY 6, 2015. You are pink and wrinkled with long, skinny legs. From a tiny poppy seed to six pounds, three ounces. Good work!

Your birthday will be sort of merged with the July 4th holiday, but that's pretty cool, I think, because of all the firecrackers involved.

When I woke up on your birthday, Uncle Ziggy and Grandpa Al were drinking coffee in our kitchen. That's because Sammy had driven Mama to the hospital in the middle of the night. They told me what was going on. Uncle Ziggy said Mama had an easy time because you were in such a hurry to be born.

I adore your name. I approved of it right away.

Mary Joy.

Mary after the famous lawyer Mary Bonauto, who made most of those Supreme Court justices understand about marrying a person you love.

And Joy because that's what our hearts are bursting with.

Mama says you are our very own Sundae Monday Mary Joy.

Dear You.

Dear Mary Joy.

Sammy helped me hang up a huge life-size poster of Steph Curry so you can see it from your crib. He sure doesn't look short! And with your own long, skinny legs, GUESS WHAT?

You will soon be a Splash Sister-in-Training, Mary Joy. (If you want to be.)

Love,

Penelope

SUNDAY, AUGUST 23, 2015

Dear Mary Joy,

You have a good pair of lungs. You kept us up last night. Mama says we don't need sleep because we are fueled by joy.

You were probably excited and overtired because of what happened yesterday.

THE WEDDING! You were there, but, of course, you won't remember anything. So I will now write about that beautiful day.

Our little backyard was jam-packed with guests. There were five big tables covered with white cloths. The party was small, but actually fancy-schmancy. We had a flute player and a violin player and a cello player, Uncle Ziggy's friends from the Oakland Secret Stairway Society, serenading us with classical music. By the way, I never heard from the Doppel Country Cousins Trio, but it doesn't matter anymore.

Uncle Ziggy was a Universal Life minister, appointed for that day only so he could marry Mama and Sammy. I'm glad it was for one day only, because he wasn't acting like Uncle Ziggy. He was so solemn, checking his notes and mumbling to himself before the ceremony.

But then, after he married Mama and Sammy, he picked up his ukulele and sang. His beautiful voice touched everyone's heart, and so did the song, called "The Book of Love." I could tell, because there were gallons of tears.

Sammy said one of her very wise things during her wedding toast. She said that love is a sixth sense. The very second we are born, we know how to love. Maybe even before that, in the womb. And love is not that complicated.

I can already tell that you are using all of your six senses with all of your baby might. You can see, hear, feel, taste, smell, and love. You loved being passed around from one guest to another, showing off your brand-new smile.

The food was catered by Gabby's aunty Lue. Gabby was right. The hors d'oeuvres were the best part. I ate many, many tiny spring rolls and mini quiches. I was too stuffed for the main course, which was Chicken Dijonnaise with mustard seeds.

And the cake!!!!!

Two layers were chocolate, two layers were strawberry, and two layers were made with the acorn flour that Mele Grace and Mele Lorraine and I bought at the Oakland Natural Co-op and gave to Aunty Lue. I wish we could have collected and used our own acorns, but that is a future project. Anyway, acorns are out of season.

The two tiny, joyful plastic brides on top of the cake were supposed to be Mama and Sammy. Everyone clapped and cheered when Mama and Sammy cut the first slice. Everyone knew that the cake and the wedding and our family, all of it, was absolutely just right.

Love,

Penelope

WHO AND WHAT I LOVE

You

Mama and Sammy

My relatives

My friends

Mr. Chen

The Golden State Warriors

My city, Oakland

The Ohlone basket

Golden retrievers

Rain

Hors d'oeuvres

Writing in my journal

Much more

MONDAY, AUGUST 24, 2015

Dear Mary Joy,

I have been thinking.

I am so glad I decided to tell you about my world while you were floating around inside your own tiny dark one.

But my world is your world now.

There are so many words in this world. I will teach you thousands and thousands of them.

Our world is awesome and ordinary
and sweet and bitter
and simple and complicated
and ancient and young
all at the very same time.

Sometimes, one word cancels out another word. I wonder a lot about that.

Soon, you will have your own journal for wondering about things. There are three dog notebooks left in Mama's desk drawer: a Pekingese and a beagle and a German shepherd.

So, from now on, I will write mostly for me, OK?

Love, always and forever,

Penelope

AUTHOR'S NOTE

The Golden State Warriors' win (June 16, 2015); the big, peaceful Oakland parade to celebrate that win (June 19, 2015); and the historic US Supreme Court decision ending same-sex marriage bans nationwide (June 26, 2015), all linked so closely in time, stirred me like a musical harmony in a love song. This story is the result of that resonance.

California droughts come and go, and, I should note, so do NBA Championships. But I hope we will continue to support and enjoy our favorite sports teams, as well as respect the environment, honor our histories, and protect all of our beautiful freedoms.

ACKNOWLEDGMENTS

I would like to give very special thanks to Corrina Gould of the Confederated Villages of Lisjan, activist and educator in Ohlone culture for fourth and fifth graders, California Indian Living program, Oakland Museum of California; Eva Herzer of the Mediation Law Office of Eva Herzer; the fascinating and oh-so-kid-friendly Oakland Museum of California; Linda Yamane, renowned Ohlone basket weaver, for her beautiful basket in the museum; and Heather Siglin, Will Osser, Griffin Osser, and Jasper Osser (and their goats!).

To everyone else who answered my questions, submitted to interviews, read my manuscript, and provided support and erudite input, I am deeply indebted: Jane Bahk; Yusni Bakar, Family Programs Director at Our Family Coalition; Phil Bildner; Claire Blethrow; Diane Bomberg; Michaela Cains; Sadie Crawford; Jordan Davis; Lola Dvorak; Madelena Fleury; Erin Harrell; Frances Hornstein; Eli Hudson; Isaac Hudson; Sarah Hudson; Ji-li Jiang; Kevin Lewis; Alia Mesker-Irwin; Serik Mesker-Irwin; Susan Meyers; Arlene Moscovitch; Aliyah Romero; Amara Romero; Erica Silverman; Ara Therrell; Anika Thielbar; Lora Thielbar; Linda Torn; Bob Unger; Gracie Wetzel; Isa Wetzel; and Greta Wu.

Many thanks to my dear, smart agent, Erin Murphy, and all the wonderful people at the Erin Murphy Literary Agency; to my incredibly wise editors, Susan Van Metre and Maggie Lehrman; to Lucy Knisley, an amazing illustrator; to Siobhán Gallagher, the book's talented designer; and to all the hardworking folks at Abrams.

Thank you and much love to my family for their input and encouragement: Rupa Basu, Arjun Basu Silverberg, Ravi Basu Silverberg, Karen Gaiger, Sarah Jackson, Leo Jackson Silverberg, Rosie Jackson Silverberg, Gerry Nelson, Eric Silverberg, and, especially, Michael Silverberg.

AND, of course, to the NBA, above all, the Golden State Warriors—

THANK YOU from the bottom of my heart!!!!!!!!!!!!!!! (Exclamation points to the nth degree.)

ANSWERS TO BASKETBALL QUIZZES

JUNE 4, 2015, GAME ONE, NBA FINALS V CLEVELAND CAVALIERS

1. Warriors, 108–100; 2. LeBron James, 44; 3. He left the Cavs for the Heat; 4. Warriors; 5. Klay Thompson; 6. Toss-up

JUNE 7, 2015, GAME TWO, NBA FINALS V. CLEVELAND CAVALIERS

1. Cavaliers, 95–93; 2. Warriors: Klay Thompson, Cavaliers: LeBron James; 3. Injured players; 4. Draymond Green; 5. Overtime; 6. Matthew Dellavedova

JUNE 9, 2015, GAME THREE, NBA FINALS V CLEVE-LAND CAVALIERS

1. Cavaliers, 96–91; 2. This is a trick question! The Cleveland Cavaliers have never won an NBA Championship. But 51 years ago, in 1964, the Cleveland Browns won the National FOOTBALL League championship. (Note from author: The Cavs won the NBA Championship in 2016!); 3. 40; 4. Points—Warriors: Curry, Cavs: James; Assists—Warriors: Curry, Cavs: James; 5. 20; 6. Five three-pointers

JUNE 11, 2015, GAME FOUR, NBA FINALS V. CLEVE-
LAND CAVALIERS

1. Warriors, 103–82; 2. No team has won a championship when they were behind 3–1 in the finals (Note from
the author: until the following season!) ; 3. Andre Iguodala;
4. Scored four three-pointers and played great defense
against James.

JUNE 16, 2015, GAME SIX, NBA FINALS V CLEVELAND
CAVALIERS

1. Warriors, 105–97; 2. Warriors; 3. Iguodala, Curry,
Thompson; 4. Iguodala; 5. Warriors!; 6. WARRIORS!!!

BOOKS AND OTHER READING MATERIAL

Bay Area News Group. *Golden Boys: The Golden State
Warriors' Historic 2015 Championship Season*. Chicago:
Triumph Books, 2015.

Bean, Lowell John, ed. *The Ohlone Past and Present:
Native Americans of the San Francisco Bay Region*. Menlo
Park, CA: Ballena Press, 1994.

Di Giacomo, Richard. *Ohlone Teacher's Resource*, 3rd
edition. CreateSpace Independent Publishing Platform,
2016.

Fakhrid-Deen, Tina; with COLAGE. *Let's Get This*

Straight: The Ultimate Handbook for Youth with LGBTQ Parents. Berkeley, CA: Seal Press, 2010.

Fleming, Charles. *Secret Stairs: East Bay: A Walking Guide to the Historic Staircases of Berkeley and Oakland*. Solana Beach, CA: Santa Monica Press, 2011.

Garner, Abigail. *Families Like Mine: Children of Gay Parents Tell It Like It Is*. New York: Harper Perennial, 2005.

Kettels, Yvonne. *Rainbow Families Coloring Book*. U.S.: Ink Works, 2012.

King, Jr., Martin Luther. "The Future of Integration." Speech delivered in Finney Chapel, Oberlin College: Oberlin, Ohio, October 22, 1964.

Margolin, Malcolm. *The Ohlone Way: Indian Life in the San Francisco–Monterey Bay Area*, 4th edition. Berkeley, CA: Heyday Books, 2014.

Murkoff, Heidi, and Sharon Mazel. *What to Expect When You're Expecting*. New York: Workman Publishing, 2008.

Solomon, Marc. *Winning Marriage: The Inside Story of How Same-Sex Couples Took on the Politicians and Pundits—and Won*. Lebanon, NH: University Press of New England, 2014.

VanDerbeken, Jaxon. "Volunteers Pitching in to Restore Wetlands," *San Francisco Chronicle*, November 16, 2014.

Wahls, Zach; with Bruce Littlefield. *My Two Moms: Lessons of Love, Strength, and What Makes a Family*. New York: Gotham Books, 2012.

News from Native California (magazine). Berkeley, CA: Heyday, 2016.

Also check out the sports section of the *East Bay Times*, especially articles by Daniel Brown, Chris De Benedetti, David DeBolt, Tom Lochner, Rebecca Parr, Mark Purdy, Carl Steward, and Marcus Thompson II.

INTERNET AND FILM

Adam Charles Bad Wound. "Acorn Song Honoring the Plants and Trees by the Costanoan Rumsen Carmel Tribe." Video, 2:07, 2017. youtube.com/watch?v=ujVCNTO -ork.

Jr. NBA. "How to Play Basketball HORSE," jr.nba.com /how-to-play-horse/.

Oakland Museum of California. "The Ohlone Basket Project: Recreating Ohlone History." Video, 1:56, 2010. youtube.com/watch?v=sC-r9vqZ00k&.

Ortiz, Beverly R., *Ohlone Curriculum with Bay Miwok Content and Introduction to Delta Yokuts.* East Bay Regional Park District, 2015. ebparks.org/activities/educators /Ohlone_Curriculum.

Poor News Network/Prensa POBRE. "Corrina Gould: On the Desecration of Ohlone Shellmounds." Video, 7:14, 2011. youtube.com/watch?v=O-epg_5Mo6s.

Provoost, Veerle. "Do Kids Think of Sperm Donors

as Family?" Video, 12:26, 2016. ted.com/talks/veerle
_provoost_do_kids_think_of_sperm_donors_as_family.
That's a Family! What Kids Want Us to Know about What
"Family" Means Today. Chasnoff, Debra, San Francisco,
CA: GroundSpark, 2000.

Also visit NBA.com for names of players and their posi-
tions and stats.

SONGS

Merritt, Stephen. "The Book of Love," performed by
Peter Gabriel on Scratch My Back (Real World/Virgin:
2010).
David, Hal, and Burt Bacharach. "What the World
Needs Now," This Is Jackie DeShannon (Imperial Re-
cords: 1965).

ORGANIZATIONS

COLAGE (Children of Lesbians and Gays Everywhere)
3815 S. Othello Street, Suite 100, #310
Seattle, WA 98118
828-782-1938
colage.org

National Basketball Association
NBA.com

National Junior Basketball

NJBL.org

Our Family Coalition: Supporting Equity for All Families
and Children

1385 Mission Street, Suite 340

San Francisco, 94103

415-981-1960

ourfamily.org

PFLAG (formerly Parents, Families, and Friends of
Lesbians and Gays)

1828 L Street, NW, Suite 660

Washington, DC 20036

202-467-8180

pflag.org

Sogorea Te' Land Trust

California Indian Environmental Alliance-CIEA

P.O. Box 2128

Berkely, CA 94702

sogoreatelandtrust@gmail.com

sogoreate-landtrust.org

The Oakland Museum of California

1000 Oak Street

Oakland, CA 94607

510-318-8400

museumca.org